The Woman
Who Stole My Life

By
Denise Shaw

Grosvenor House
Publishing Limited

The right of Denise Shaw to be identified as the author of this
work has been asserted in accordance with Section 78
of the Copyright, Designs and Patents Act 1988

The book cover is copyright to Denise Shaw
Cover image copyright to Vitality Art

This book is published by
Grosvenor House Publishing Ltd
Link House
140 The Broadway, Tolworth, Surrey, KT6 7HT.
www.grosvenorhousepublishing.co.uk

This is a work of fiction. Unless otherwise indicated,
all the names, characters businesses, places, events and incidents
in this book are either the product of the author's imagination
or used in fictitious manner. Any resemblance to actual persons,
living or dead, or actual events is purely coincidental.

A CIP record for this book
is available from the British Library

ISBN 978-1-80381-912-9

For my children and grandchildren —
you have my heart

Special Thanks

With special thanks to Melanie Bartle, Publishing Administrator of Grosvenor House Publishing, for all her help and expertise with making my story a reality.

Prologue

I am led into a dingy airless room and am asked to take a seat. Looking around me, I note that there is only one window in the room, and it is very dirty. I cannot tell if the dirt is on the inside or out; I suspect that it is both. Although the window is quite large, there is only one small window at the top that can be opened. I assume that this is to prevent any criminals from making their getaway. I imagine myself throwing a brick through the large pane of glass so that I can make my escape. I can vaguely make out the carpark at the rear of the police station and can picture me jumping into a car and driving away at speed, distancing myself from this situation, but where would I go?

I feel like I am not really in the room, but am observing the proceedings from outside of myself. I do know, though, that my real self is sat facing two police officers. One is a big man with huge shoulders and an equally big voice. Everything about him is imposing, it feels like he is taking up more space in the small interview room than is strictly necessary. I stare at his arms and I think to myself that I expect he works out and spends every evening at the gym. I bet his wife is fed up with it; I know that I would be. I wonder if he takes steroids and I almost laugh to myself. Of course, he cannot be, he is an upstanding member of the law.

Then I recall my father saying that the police cannot be trusted any more than anybody else, that inside the uniform they are the same as the rest of us. I am ashamed to say that I was brought up with the general notion that you mistrust them first and tell them nothing, second. My father had a close relationship with a police constable friend, and they used to do 'jobs' together, none of which were legitimate. This friend was as crooked and slippery as any member of the criminal fraternity.

As this man is such a formidable character, I find that my hands have gone clammy and my forehead is perspiring. I really pray that my sweat does not drop onto the table as I will be so embarrassed. My heart is beating extremely fast, it feels as if it is almost bursting out of my chest. This would not be a suitable time to have a panic attack but, dear God, now I feel like laughing. This happens to me often; I always want to laugh at inappropriate times. For example, if somebody really hurts themselves, or if they are delivering some devastating news. This can be exacerbated by their expression, please try not to look too serious or I may crack.

However, he is staring at me so sternly, that I dare not laugh, in fact, I dare not even move. I stare down at the Formica-topped table and notice that it is pale green and is quite chipped at the edges. *Very 1970s*, I remember thinking to myself. This is what they call 'retro'. I ponder as to how much it would sell for at auction, or on one of those dreadful daytime TV shows, where they like to 'upcycle' or 'shabby chic' someone's home. In my head, I change that to 'shabby shit'. I am in danger of completely losing it, in a minute. I need to sort out my attitude and try to look suitably contrite. This is difficult, as I am not, nor never will be, sorry.

Due to my recent adult diagnosis of ADHD, or attention deficit hyperactivity disorder, to give it its proper title (and to be honest this has been a gift), I now understand why I have felt so 'different' to everybody else for my entire life. Why I cannot stand being in a room of people chatting – whose conversation should I listen to? Why does all the noise hurt my head and set my teeth on edge? Why at school I could not concentrate and why my school reports always mentioned my 'looking out of the window, daydreaming'. Why I find it so hard to remember things, or to focus.

I am always so restless and fidgety. It drives everybody mad, including myself. I cannot stay inside for too long because, if I do, I will feel like a caged animal, who might be compelled to rip your head off. Understandably, as it now turns out, I am finding it such a strain to remain in my seat, that I want to run around this room screaming at the top of my lungs and I want to tear my own hair out. The 'head' doctor also stated that I might be inclined to be impulsive and may look at ways to increase my own dopamine levels, through risky or inappropriate behaviour. Unfortunately, that has not been enough to help me get away with this.

The sidekick to the other officer is a mousy-haired plain Jane of a woman. Her hair looks very dry. It requires a good conditioner (certainly not a cheap one) and she needs to spend some serious money to sort this problem out. It is scrunched up in a ponytail, with a couple of wispy bits on each side that have escaped their hair bobble. In my mind, I call them 'entrails'. I nearly laugh aloud, as I picture Melissa's entrails lying on the grass when I beat her to death. I fantasize for a few moments about what I have done and relive the pleasure of hearing the relentless thudding noise as I hit her repeatedly with the piece of wood.

The female officer looks timid and at complete odds with her position. She wears no make-up, though her cheeks look ruddy in complexion. I think that she has spent a great deal of time outdoors – on a farm? I imagine her with horses as she is a horsey type. I wonder if her appearance would improve with a makeover and decide that it absolutely could. She has never been married (I would be surprised if she has ever been kissed). I then feel genuinely sorry for her, as I cannot imagine having never been kissed, or never ever having experienced some really pleasurable, rampant, and uninhibited sex. I picture in my mind me and Frank having sex and it takes all the strength that I have not to break down there and then. I make a determined effort to swallow and hold back the tears that are threatening to spring from my eyes. I am so, so tired of this emotional pain.

She is not going to understand any part of my story. How can she? She is not qualified. Only somebody that has loved like I have, or who has hated like I have, would appreciate what Frank and Melissa have done to me. 'Mouse', as I have now named her in my mind, looks at me over the top of her glasses and then periodically looks down to read her notes. I try to read her writing upside down, but I do not have my glasses (it was the last thing I thought about when I was arrested). Her writing is illegible. Even this annoys me. How is she going to know what she has written? Does she have no pride in her work?

The male officer introduces himself as Detective Chief Inspector John Campbell He has a broad Scottish accent. I am already worrying as to whether I will be able to understand him. 'Mouse' introduces herself as Detective Constable Beryl Symons. My solicitor has already advised me to say 'no comment' to everything that I am going to be asked but, at this stage, I no longer care what happens to me, as *she* stole my life and I have taken immense pleasure in taking hers.

***

You must understand that I did not plan to kill her. But I did have a burning desire to punish her for what she had done to me and to my family. It was not so much retribution. I simply wanted to balance the scales of justice. You see, Melissa was like a black widow spider. She caught men in her web of deceit and false promises. She lured them in, using all of her powers of seduction. Oh, she was good! I had seen this play out in front of my own eyes. I could only watch her in sheer wonderment, and with a little bit of admiration, to be honest, as she had expertly honed her craft. But, like a fly in her web, she devoured men alive, and these men, well, these men, they did not see what was happening until it was too late.

I felt Melissa had gotten away with destroying people's lives for too long, and for what? A kind of game? A sport? Just because she could? I tried to make sense of it in my mind, but I could not, as I would never deliberately hurt another human being, so you might wonder, therefore, if I am sorry I killed her, when I have just told you that I could never deliberately hurt another human being. Certainly not. She was practically begging for it and I was extremely happy to oblige. I only wished I had done it sooner.

Chapter 1

Following my sentencing and my subsequent incarceration, I have had a great deal of time to reflect upon what I have done. In fact, at my final sentencing, when the judge summed up what he thought about my actions and spoke of Melissa's 'terribly sad and tragic demise' he also said something like (as I was not really listening)' "I find the defendant devoid of any emotions." Which is ironic, really, but more of that later… He also said that *I* had a 'callous disregard for human life' and that *I* had spared no thought for my victim! He did not have a clue.

I had done nothing but think about this woman for an entire year! I could not eat, sleep or breathe without her permeating my every thought. I found her very presence in my brain, stifling, debilitating and constant. He brought the proceedings to a conclusion by asking me to consider carefully what I had done and hoped that, in time, I would feel some sorrow, sympathy and deep regret. For however long I remain in this hellhole, his wishes are going to be totally and spectacularly disregarded. Forever. You try to live a 'normal' life, judge, after you have walked a mile in my shoes. Honestly, Melissa was enough to make a saint switch sides.

If any of you are wondering how I sleep at night, I sleep like a contented baby, thank you. Okay, so it is a bit noisy in here, with people shouting, keys jangling and metal doors slamming, but that is all external, I can block it out. But, inside my head, where it matters, for the first time in such a long time, my brain and its thoughts are finally free. The most pressing thing I must worry about now is will the toast still be crispy by the time I join the breakfast queue in the morning, or is it going to be soggy or rubbery like it was yesterday? I do not think about Melissa at all now. I have managed to quieten all that anger, paranoia and suffering. She no longer tries to worm her way into my consciousness. In more ways than one, Melissa is dead, and I am not going to lie to you, it is absolutely, bloody fantastic!

To understand my story absolutely, I am going to have to take you right back to the very beginning. The events that shaped me and the consequences that followed. I know that you are going to find it hard to accept that murder can, or ever should, be justified. You have already concluded in your mind that I am a cold, hard-hearted killer, or a psychopath, but we all have our limits and let me tell you what caused me to reach the end of mine. It is a long story, but please bear with me. And what I did, well, it had been a long time coming, and I never thought that it would end like this, not in a million years. I have discovered that not all is fair in love and judging. And that was why I was able to state with absolute conviction, "Not guilty, m'lud."

***

I first met my husband, Frank, at an antenatal class 31 years ago. He was there with his then wife, Sharon, and they were expecting their first baby. I was there with my husband, Tom, and we were also expecting our first baby. It is incredible, really, how life events happen and why you cross some people's paths at certain times, and why. And how some seemingly insignificant events have an enormous impact on your life numerous years later. Who would have predicted that 11 years later, and with a second child each, that Frank and I would end up being together?

In my 56 years of life experience thus far, I have observed that in every couple, one person will love the other a little bit more. When I tell people this – because, if nothing else, I am unashamedly honest – they usually look at me quizzically with their head cocked to one side and then I watch their eyes glaze over. I am sure they think I am cuckoo. However, they all, without exception, start thinking about which way round it is in their case, and they usually are not overly enamoured with the result, particularly if it does not favour them. It was like that for me and Frank. I always knew that I loved him a little bit more than he loved me. Now I even wonder if he ever loved me at all. But I thought that I loved him enough for both of us, so I stupidly thought it would somehow balance out in the end. As far as 'red flags' go, I am the queen of totally ignoring all of them.

I also believe that it is extremely rare to find the one true love of your life. I think some people never get to meet 'their' person as for some reason their paths do not ever get to cross or fate, and timing have other ideas. I *know* that Frank was the love of my life. If I was not in so much emotional pain, I would be thankful that I had experienced it. You might think that I have been blessed or lucky? But, no, you would be wrong, because losing Frank has been the hardest, most harrowing, and most devastating loss that I have ever had to endure.

I am not going to lie to you, but when I was in Frank's arms, everything felt right and complete with the world. He made me feel the most secure I had ever felt, I felt protected from any cruelties the world could throw at me. He was my 'coming home'. He was my safe place. I still had that feeling of excitement and anticipation when I heard his car pull into the drive when he finished work each evening. And 18 years later my stomach could still produce 'butterflies' if I looked at him across a crowded room. I loved him passionately, totally and completely unconditionally. I am genuinely sorry if you have not ever experienced this, but on the upside, and there is an upside to everything, it will save you heartache later, should anything ever go wrong. And at least Melissa cannot destroy your life, like she destroyed mine. Yes, I have seen to that, and you're very welcome.

Who would have predicted that the person that I loved so much would change so completely? That they would become my unsafe place and that they would shake the very foundations of my life and my soul. That everything I thought I knew and trusted so unreservedly would literally come crashing down like a wall at every side of me. If you had told me that Frank and I would ever 'go wrong', I would have laughed you out of the room. I thought, with some arrogance on my part, that our love was unshakeable and that we could endure anything and survive anything. I was looking forward to our retirement years, when hopefully we would be blessed with grandchildren and have time to travel and to do things together, now that our children were all grown and were living their own lives. Oh, how my dreams were to be so devastatingly shattered into tiny little pieces.

In 2005, *I* proposed to Frank on the London Eye. It was exciting and romantic, and I totally surprised him. I was taking a risk as neither of us was divorced from our previous partners at this point and it felt as though we were rushing things.

But I was so sure about us that I felt it was a risk I was willing to take. ADHD has always made me more than a little reckless and I have always let my feelings dictate my path, without engaging my brain (which is not just reckless, it is also stupid). But! I wanted to be Frank's wife and I would have given him the world. He accepted, and we had a wonderful evening, and I genuinely thought that I could never be happier than I was in that moment. In marrying, I would feel secure at last. It would properly make us part of each other's lives, and of each other's families. We would be bringing our children together and creating our own little family. He with his children, Tilly and Bradley, and me with James and Rosie, and I could not wait to begin our new life.

After Frank and I got together, I remember writing a letter to Frank's parents, telling them that I would look after him and that I totally adored him. Frank had previously told me how devastated they were about his and Sharon's marriage ending. I also promised them that I would love and take care of their grandchildren to the best of my ability, because I knew how worried they must have been. They did not really know me or what I would be like being a new step-parent in their grandchildren's lives. If I promise something, I will try extremely hard to fulfil what I have promised. Frank and all our four children were now central to the whole of my life, and I did not really care about anything else.

Mine and Frank's sex life was completely insane. I could not get enough of him, in fact, we could not get enough of each other. We 'christened' every room of the house. To me, he was like some kind of weird hypnotic drug that I had to have to survive. We had sex on the sofa, on the stairs, up against the wall... You name it, we did it. I am sure we even did it on the kitchen table.

It was brilliant (I had thought until this point, that multiple orgasms were just a myth). We took a year off work, which is just as well, as we did not have time to live a 'normal' life. We wondered, in fact, how we would ever go back to a 'normal' life after what we were experiencing. We were constantly tired.

Lust is an enormously powerful drug. That is what it was, I know that now. I once ripped a shirt clean off his back and the buttons flew off and scattered all over the floor. We could not keep our hands off each other, even in the supermarket. It certainly made shopping trips less dull. Frank worked as a self-employed lorry driver at this time, and he was able to employ another person to work for him, whilst still getting paid. So, for an entire year, we stayed in bed. A year! Not just 'nine-and-a-half weeks' (that film had nothing on us…). We would only get out of bed to use the loo, or to get food for sustenance. Our snack of choice was usually crackers with cheese and pickled onions, or pâté. There was no time to cook.

If we were looking after the children, we obviously did not behave like that. But if we had visitors and *had to* get dressed, we would both be clock-watching and hoped that they would not stay long. Sunday afternoons were our very favourite day of the week, and we would look forward to it all week, knowing that we were going to have a huge sex marathon once we were child-free. I am sorry if you do not want to read about this, but I have already told you that I am unashamedly honest (which is to my detriment as you are now thinking that I am some kind of deranged sex addict). So we had – what I thought was – as near to a perfect life as you could get. However, I did used to think to myself, *This cannot go on indefinitely, it is too good.* But I shut that thought out. When was I going to learn to listen to my internal voice?

Before we married, we lived in a rented house in Plymouth. It was a horrible house, I hated it. I cannot go past it now without feeling sick. It brings back terrible memories of the extremely challenging times trying to get the children to settle. James and Rosie missed their dad terribly and Rosie in particular, found it difficult having another father figure telling her what to do, which understandably caused friction. We had Frank's children, Tilly and Bradley, every weekend and then we had to adjust to being a family of six. Of course, Tilly and Bradley were jealous of the time Frank now spent with my children. It was around this time that Frank suggested we just buggered off somewhere and bought two tickets. Again, a massive metaphorical red flag could have detached from a mast in the wind and blown across my face, but *still* I ignored it. I told him that I could *never* leave my children, not in a month of Sundays and was internally appalled that he felt able or willing to leave his.

It is not easy taking on other people's children, as I soon found out. They were all struggling with their parents no longer being together, adjusting to a new type of family situation and having to accept a new parent, whom they may or may not even like. You may not like your stepchildren and if you are taking the time to read this, remember that those children share 50 percent of your partner's DNA, so you should, and can, love them. How could you not? If you did not, wouldn't it mean that you did not really love your partner? But I was fortunate, I really loved (and still do) Tilly and Bradley. And I honestly believed that Frank loved me and my children like that.

We decided to marry in the Bahamas, just the two of us. I did not want the traditional wedding this time, as it did not feel appropriate. I am quite old-fashioned and did not think it was right as we had both meant our wedding vows the first time but had clearly messed up. I felt upset for Frank's mother when we were leaving, as she said that she would have really liked to have been there for the wedding; and that was the one and only time when I worried that we had done the wrong thing, going off on our own. We promised our children that we would all go on holiday together once we came back, which we did – we took them camping in France.

Frank had bought an 'all inclusive' wedding package, so everything that we needed would be supplied when we got there. We were given our own little apartment, which was really pretty and was set in a lovely location of trees and flowers. There was a mini hot tub in the gardens, which we enjoyed spending time in, and all around the site there were different themed restaurants, so you could go anywhere to eat, ranging from an American diner to a fresh fish restaurant, where you could watch them cook in front of you on a massive hot plate. We had arrived on the tail end of hurricane season, so it was quite windy and not amazingly hot but, from what I can remember, it was pleasantly warm and sunny. The whole thing was like a dream, it felt surreal. We were in love, in a stunning location and we, again, had more than our fair share of sex, but this time on a massive queen-sized bed (once we had moved the towels that were folded into swans).

A few days before our wedding, Frank broke his foot jumping out of his lorry and spent a night in hospital. So we were not sure if we would be able to fly, as he had to wear one of those surgical boots. But it turned out to be a blessing as we had special treatment at the airport and transport for us and our suitcases. It was genuine fun to whizz past everyone else who was walking. Moving away from tradition again, Frank wore shorts and I wore a bikini on our wedding day. The staff could not believe that I had not brought a dress with me! We had planned to marry on the beach, but it was so windy that we got married under a pergola in one of the gardens, but it was still a beautiful setting.

Although the Bahamas is not in the Bible Belt, the people there are predominantly Christian, so our pastor had prayed the night before for guidance as to what he should say at our wedding. Unfortunately, all I can remember him saying was that he hoped that God would bless our union and that he knew that we had both been through tough times to get where we were today. Frank (who was not one to show much outward emotion) and I cried with the sheer magnitude of the occasion. I found it so difficult to talk, as I loved Frank so much and I meant my vows, absolutely, no matter what.

Please do not think I did not mean them the first time. I did, but Tom and I were so young when we married, and we were both very damaged from our own difficult childhoods. I do not think we fully realized the enormity of our vows and, in retrospect, I really needed counselling, because of my childhood trauma. But my first broken marriage still saddens me to this day and makes me feel like a failure. I never ever wanted to be divorced and I am mostly responsible for the breakdown of my first marriage ,and for that I am terribly sorry. But at the time of my marriage to Frank, I was 37 and I knew exactly what I had signed up for.

Chapter 2

You need to know a bit about my childhood to better understand me. I will go back to my marriage to Frank at the right time. Well, quite honestly, it is a wonder that I am not insane. You are thinking that I am, what with me killing Melissa and everything, but when I killed her, it felt like the only truly rational thing I have ever done. And, to be honest, I am really, really pleased that I had the balls to do it.

***

My parents were just an average kind of couple. They met in the '60s in a stationery factory. Dad was on the shop floor, and my mother was a telephonist. My dad said that my mother was the most beautiful woman he had ever seen. When drivers passed her, they nearly crashed their cars, so the story goes, and he had once seen a man walk into a lamp post because he was so busy staring at her across the street. Obviously, I was not there, so have nothing to verify his account, but I do have the wedding photos and she was, in my opinion, extremely attractive. Anyway, she got pregnant, and they ended up having a shotgun wedding (the shame of being an unmarried mother in the '60s was far too much of an idea for either of their families to entertain).

I was the happy result, and I am being sarcastic here. My mother was only 20 at the time, and dad was 23. My mother told me in later years that she just could not cope with the responsibility of it all. They had a baby, a mortgage and had an ill-judged marriage that they had rushed. She told me that she spent her 21st birthday crying because I was crying and she had run out of ideas of how to soothe me. She was handwashing terry towelling nappies that day because they did not have a washing machine and then her mother came around for a visit and criticised her for the nappies not being very white! Why could she have not given the poor girl a break?

Dad worked three jobs to make ends meet, so Mum spent hours on her own. Also (back to one person loving the other person more than the other one), she barely loved him and he adored her. Well, it was bound to go wrong, wasn't it? My dad was a stickler for anyone down on their luck. Many a Christmas was spent when I was growing up with the odd tramp at our house being invited to dinner, or anyone at all who did not have anywhere else to go. The number of people invited was a surprise every year. There was always an eclectic mix of characters, from dodgy police officers to criminals who had just been released from prison (we had a man come to stay once who nicked all my jewellery and my dad's wages). So, when I was three and he met a new man at work who had just come out of prison, my dad said that of course he could lodge with them. It would be an act of favour for them too, as they would get extra income from it, so it was to be a mutually beneficial relationship.

This would have all been very tickety-boo had the lodger not looked like a Greek god, with long curly brown hair, piercing blue eyes, sun-kissed skin and a way of charming the ladies. He was also a bit 'edgy' as he had 'done time' (show me a woman who does not like a bad boy, and I will show you a liar). Also, my maternal grandfather was a policeman and as my mum also took pleasure from rebelling against authority, it was a match made in heaven. My mum could sing a bit and had long legs and a good figure; she had once auditioned to be in Pan's People, who were a British female dance troupe in the '60s and '70s. Well, Rob, the lodger, stroked her ego (and other things) and told her that he had 'connections' and that he could make her a 'star'. You can see why her head was turned. It must have been such a heady concoction that I cannot find it in me to criticise her, because I totally understand how it happened, I really do.

The next part of this story is going to sound a bit far-fetched, but I promise that what I am telling you is the truth. Firstly, it will be no surprise to you that Rob and my mother decided to do a bunk, taking me with them. Unbeknown to my mum, Rob was a wanted man and was about to be arrested for further criminal activities. What these 'activities' were, I cannot tell you, as I have never been told, but it must have been quite serious because of what happened next. My mum's friend, Denise, who worked next to her as a telephonist – and whom I was named after – was somehow part of this ménage à trois (and I am not sure in what capacity), but the four of us were about to run away to Ireland.

I can still distinctly remember being on the ferry with Rob, my mother, and Denise. I can recall watching a black and white screening of *Tom and Jerry* whilst eating a boiled egg with dippy soldiers. I remember many lights as we were entering the boat. I was three years old. I remember all of this because I did not feel safe, and the memories still fill me with abject fear. Where was my daddy? Where were we going? I was terrified. I had previously been on a bus with Rob and my mother, in the days when you could smoke on a bus, and Rob thought it was funny to use my hand as an ashtray. I remember my mum laughing and I remember crying and finding the ash hot as it landed in my palm. For several years, I had recurring dreams of the lights and of the feeling of being out of control. I am still very scared of being in the dark, being alone and being vulnerable, in fact I really detest it.

Apart from one memory of being on a balcony with my mother and Denise, I have no other recollection of anything that happened, or of where we were staying, but I have learned since that we were living in Dublin. I still have my paternal grandmother's diary from this time and have gleaned some of what happened from that. On January 22nd 1970, my grandmother had written the following: 'We heard today that you are "lost" darling, somewhere with your mother and her lover. But not lost to God, His wings stretch wide. Console your father one day for the agony of this day. He tried so hard and loves you so much'.

I have been told that, Denise, who must have had a pang of conscience and had thought that she was becoming too entrenched in this child abduction, telephoned the police back in the UK and informed them of what they had done, The Irish Gardaí came to arrest them as my mother had taken me without my father's consent. Rob was arrested and was promptly escorted back to the UK (I do not know what happened to Denise). Myself and my mother were placed into the care of the convent of the Redemptoristine Nuns in Saint Alphonsus' Monastery in Dublin. I have no recollection of this, but my mum always said that the nuns were really kind to us.

We stayed there whilst social services in the UK were contacted to plan for me to be taken into care. But first I was taken to a police station in England whilst they waited for my allocated social worker to arrive. I was on my own now. I did not know where my mother or my father was. This part contains a very vivid memory. The police officer assigned to look after me was really kind, warm and jolly. I remember being hungry and he asked what I would like to eat, so I asked for a jam sandwich, which he dutifully had made for me with soft white bread, but whoever made it had not cut the crusts off! So, when he left the room and I had eaten the 'good' bit, I stuffed the crusts down the back of the chair, so that he would not find them and would think that I had eaten them. He declared, "You are such a good girl to eat all your sandwiches!" (I did not stop cutting the crusts off my sandwiches until I was about 13 years old when I found it embarrassing to do so in front of my friends).

We lived in Dublin for five months! This is another excerpt from my grandmother's diary: 'You were missing for five months, my darling. May you never know the agony or anxiety your father or your grandparents suffered. People were praying for your safe return, not only in the UK, but in India, in Rome and in Africa!'.

The social worker assigned to me and tasked with taking me to my paternal grandparents' house gives me a warm memorable feeling of being so pleased to see them and finally feeling safe. My social worker (I so wish I could recall her name) was an extremely tall lady and my grandmother said that my first words were, "This lady is as tall as the sky!" When my father heard that I was back, he ran home from work, picked me up and swung me around. Years later, my nanna told me that she could not bear to watch the ending of *The Railway Children* because the end scene, when the father returns from the war and the children run up to him at the railway station, took her right back to that very moment.

Chapter 3

Once I was taken back to the UK, I initially stayed with my paternal grandparents. Social services let me stay there temporarily as my grandparents had agreed to look after me while my fate was decided. I do not have any recollection of staying with them, and the subsequent events I have learned only from what I have been told. Rob was awaiting trial and my mother was staying with her own parents at this time. Social services had numerous meetings and after a short while I was moved yet again, this time to be with my mother who was living with her parents, on the proviso that she did not make any contact with Rob.

I loved my maternal grandmother very much, but she was a difficult woman. She could be really kind, warm and affectionate one minute and then suddenly turn into a vicious harridan of a woman with a bitterness that I have never experienced in anybody else since. This caused me to be always 'quiet and good' so as not to alter the equilibrium. I was a very insecure and needy child, who needed much affection and I think that she found me suffocating. She used to say in an exasperated tone, "You are such a cuddly child!" As if it was an annoying character flaw and that used to make me feel like I was not 'normal.'

She and my mother had a very volatile relationship. It swung from being warm and loving to a shared hatred of each other. My mother once threatened to 'run a knife' right through her mother if she did not shut up. In retrospect, I really think that my grandmother had bipolar, which was not recognized back then as a mental health diagnosis. But her mother before her, my great-grandmother, was sectioned and put into a mental hospital in her 40s. She had been so disturbed that she was able to pull radiators off the walls with her bare hands if she entered a positively belligerent rage. I feel that I could do the same, if pushed far enough.

After a period of living with first my paternal grandparents and then my maternal ones, it was decided that I needed a more permanent living arrangement. My mother did not get on very well with her parents, they were always rowing and even now I cannot bear to be in a room with people shouting at each other. My mother had been sexually abused by my grandfather and, knowing this, my father decided that he would apply to the court to get custody of me. This was unheard of in the '70s, as the mother was almost always granted custody of her children, regardless of whether it would be better for the child.

My mother was advised at this time to stop her contact with Rob if she wanted any chance of winning the court case. But, unfortunately, she just could not give him up as the pull was just too strong. This, until quite recently, has had a profound effect on me. The ultimate rejection surely occurs if your own mother chooses someone else over you. It has taken me 47 years to finally forgive her. She was young, she was foolish, but she was human. 'Let he who is without sin cast the first stone' and all that. Fortunately, I am now in a better place mentally but any sort of rejection is a massive trigger for me and Frank rejecting me for Melissa was far, far worse, which I will try to explain later.

So, in a ground-breaking court case that went on for several months, my father finally won custody. It was so rare that it made the national press. Like I said previously, it was almost unprecedented that a father would gain full custody of his child. It was also decided that I would go with him to live with his parents. My paternal grandparents, Binks and Dick, were the kindest, most loving substitute parents that anybody could ever have wished for. However, it was often quite a lonely childhood, aside from when my cousins, Michael and Alison, came to stay and we always had tremendous fun together.

I always felt very 'different' from my peers though. There were not many children from divorced parents in those days and at primary school all my friends knew that I lived with my grandparents. If they asked me why, I am ashamed that to say that I said my mother was dead, as I was embarrassed that they would never get to see me with her. She was granted access to me at the weekends and often she would not arrive to pick me up. My nanna used to get me all dressed up in my 'Sunday best' and I would sit by the window waiting for her to arrive. When she did not, the atmosphere at home was palpable. My nanna was enraged, but tried to say (in a voice that did not match up with what she was saying) that my mother could not help it and that she had somehow forgotten.

In an alarming turn of events, I was once playing in the playground and my mother turned up at my school! Remember I had told all my friends that she was dead? Well, this was going to take some explaining and I cannot remember what I said to get around it. But she looked stunning. I recall her long shiny chestnut-brown hair, her mini skirt, with those long legs beneath, and her platform shoes. I did feel proud that she was mine. Anyway, she had come to say goodbye to me and said that she would not see me for a while (I did not see much of her anyway) and she said that she was moving to Jersey with her new boyfriend, John. When she met John, she wrote Rob a 'dear John' letter, while he was in prison, telling him that their relationship was over. Ironic, really.

I do not recall being upset, but I do remember my father and his parents being absolutely furious when I told them that night. The next day, my father took me to school and shouted at my teacher (whom I loved) for allowing my mother to come into the playground, let alone have a conversation with me. Then my teacher, who was only young, burst into tears and then I felt guilty for causing all this upset. Since then, I have had a constant battle with feeling guilty, even if it is not always my fault. I do wonder if this has something to do with being raised by a catholic grandmother.

My paternal grandmother's faith was strong. I went to Mass with her every Sunday and we prayed together every evening; these prayers always included ones for my mother. What a woman my grandmother was! It would have been understandable if she had hated her for what she had done. Years later, I found a letter that my mother had written to her thanking her for bringing me up so well, and she asked her to forgive her, writing that she was young and foolish at that time and had not thought about what she was doing. Although my grandmother's faith was strong and admirable, like I said, I have been carrying massive guilt for the whole of my life. Binks had a colour poster of Jesus crucified, wearing a crown of thorns on his head, with blood running down his face, on the back of her wardrobe door and she once said to me, "Every time you sin, it is like you driving one of those thorns into Jesus' head." I can only imagine what she would think of what I have done to Melissa.

Chapter 4

I stayed living with Binks, Dick, and my father until I was nine years old. Then the council rehomed my father and I, and we went to live in a two-bedroomed flat. It was a very upsetting day when I left the care of my grandparents. They and their home were all I had ever really known, and they had offered me a place of safety and security. It had not always been easy though. My nanna told anybody that was prepared to listen, that I had been a 'gift from God', that I was a 'joy to look after', that I was 'always so well behaved' and, of course, I was always 'quiet and good'. No pressure then.

Although I felt secure, I was not ever myself. I doubt that my grandparents ever knew the real me. Trust me, I am not even that nice. My real self, wanted to run and scream and misbehave, like any other regular child, but I stayed 'quiet and good'. This, after all, is what people expected of me. I was always trying so hard not to alter the equilibrium, wherever I found myself to be, or with whoever I happened to be with. This is a theme that, until recently, has shaped me and the course of my life.

Life with my father was completely different to my life with my grandparents. In fact, it could not have been more of a stark contrast. My father was a terrible womaniser. Knowing men as I do now, I guess he would have said that he was great at it! I never knew who he was going to introduce to me next. Some of the women I really liked and some of them I would have wanted to be my mum, but just as I got used to them, they would be gone and then the next one would appear. I was a 'gift' for my dad, as he used me to get women. Who would not admire a single dad who had raised a daughter by himself and then had fought for custody and won against the odds? Yes, they all thought that he was wonderful!

The reality was that he often left me for lengthy periods on my own. I did not ever know if or when he was coming back. I had gone from having three square meals a day, at regular times, to takeaways, missed meals, doughnuts and whatever I could find in the fridge. My diet with my grandparents was complimented with Haliborange vitamin C tablets to prevent colds, Metatone tonic, in case I was ever under the weather, cod liver oil, for my bones (I do not think that the cod liver oil achieved anything), and malted milk extract, for a healthy gut.

My father never lost his desire to 'rescue' people who might need him. This now mostly involved women. When I caught him in bed with the 15-year-old paper delivery girl (I can only assume that she had problems at home) I found this morally repugnant, even then, as I knew it was wrong. He also dated a prostitute for some years. She tried to 'win me over' by buying me a blue silk dress, but I knew what she was, and I was a snob even then, so, I treated her with contempt. I found a letter he had written to her, saying that he would 'take her away' from her life of meaningless sex (by giving her more meaningless sex?), and he told her that he thought she was worth more than a 'quick shag'.

Once he dated a lady in a wheelchair who was a paraplegic; she had been in a car accident when she was 19. He took great delight in acting as if he were her legs and of carrying her everywhere. Putting her on chairs and lifting her in and out of the car and being her hero. I really liked this one, notwithstanding the fact that I fancied both of her sons, for two distinct reasons. One was handsome and exotic-looking, and the other was sporty and a lot of fun. This relationship, however, was another one with not much longevity.

Despite all of this, please do not get me wrong, I really loved my dad and would have laid down and died for him if he had asked me to. Obviously, as you become older and wiser, you no longer put your parents on such a high pedestal. If you do, they are bound to fall off! As it turns out, we are all fundamentally flawed, human, and prone to make mistakes. Our own parents are no exception. Especially mine.

***

My dad only just stayed on the right side of the law and when I say 'only just', I mean that he fortunately never got caught. When I was around 11 or 12, he had to sit me down to inform me that he had been accused of stealing from work and that it was not just a little bit. He said that he stood a very good chance of being sent to prison. Happily, by luck or providence, he managed to get away with it (he told me that he had not done it, but I did not believe him). I do not know what would have become of me had he been convicted, as my grandparents were now moving to the north of England.

***

My mother did not stay in Jersey for long and afterwards moved to Whitley Bay in Tyneside to be with John, which is where he came from. By this time, she had another daughter, with John, called Fern. I was *so* jealous! My mum sent me one of those new baby announcement cards and I was devastated. I tore it up into hundreds of little bits and put it in the dustbin. I can remember crying and wondering why she was keeping this baby when she did not keep me.

I used to visit my mum, but not very often as it was a long journey from the south of England to Newcastle. Unbelievably, my dad let me go on the coach, from the age of nine, on my own, and it used to take over nine hours, including changing coaches at London Victoria. A little girl with a big suitcase must have been a remarkable sight. It seems infeasible now, that anybody would do that. Having had children myself, I cannot imagine what he was thinking.

I grew to love my baby sister. My mother went on to have two more children after that, Joy and Christian. I genuinely loved them all but, again, I was jealous as they had got to stay with our mother and I was an outsider, who did not really belong in their family dynamic. Not ever really fitting in or being part of something is another theme that has followed me throughout my life. Without the various friendship groups I have been privileged to have had in my life, I doubt that I would have been half the person that I have been. That is, until I met Melissa.

***

So, life with just me and my father was quite lonely, aside from the vast array of women that I was introduced to. Quite a few of the women had children and I would just get used to mixing with my new playmates when my father and their mother split up and we would never see each other again. My father enjoyed a relationship for some time with our next-door neighbour. I really do think that it was just a matter of convenience on his part – not having to travel very far for a sexual liaison. He did not even bother to use the stairs, simply leaping over our balcony into hers. I felt sorry for her, as I could tell that she really liked him and I got along very well with her daughter.

I do think that my father's treatment of women has tainted my view of men. I have never really trusted any man, until I trusted Frank wholeheartedly, but that is a mistake that I will not make again. Thank God I am in prison, away from their lies and their false promises of fidelity. Also, my stepbrothers, Leon and Gareth, have proven to follow in his footsteps and, as adults, I have learned a lot from them as to what makes men tick. My brother, Leon, told me once that he behaves like a perfect gentleman for several dates, pretending he is really wholesome and not ready to take a relationship to a sexual level, until the women are driven into a sexual frenzy, wondering what is wrong with them, and then they do all the seducing as they are not able to wait any longer. Clever, or what?

Just before my 13th birthday, my father met Trisha. She had just come out of a bad relationship and was quite damaged. She was incredibly attractive and delicate. I think that my father thought that she needed 'rescuing', which is something you know he liked. So, she, her two sons, a dog, and a cat, all moved in with us into our two-bedroomed flat. Talk about the sublime to the ridiculous! But at least my dad wanted to make an honest woman out of this one and they did marry the day before my 13th birthday.

My dad failed to inform the next-door neighbour that Trisha and her family were moving in and I can only imagine her hurt and surprise when she saw all the comings and goings. I felt really awful for her and guilty on my dad's behalf and, years later, tracked her down and wrote her a letter, telling her that I was so sorry for what he had done to her. He also failed to tell Trisha that he had been 'dating' a prostitute and that she had her own key to our flat. I can only imagine the surprise on her face, and that of my stepmum's, when she let herself in one morning. I would love to have been a fly on the wall during that encounter!

Anyway, I now had a mum, and I was pleased. And I have to say that, as a stepmother, Trisha was, and does, treat me like a daughter. She has taken her role extremely seriously and I have tried to emulate the love and kindness that she has shown me throughout her life when it came to the love and care of my own stepchildren, Tilly and Bradley, but considering what has happened since, I think that, unlike her, I must have failed miserably.

Chapter 5

Life with my father, Trisha, and her boys, was fairly settled. But, again, I felt like an outsider. That is in no way a reflection of how I was treated, but my dad had Trisha and Trisha had her boys, so I felt a bit like a square peg in a round hole. Trisha and my father married, so I had a stepmother at last! From then, and to the present, she could not have taken her new role more seriously. There is no doubt in my mind that she loves me as if I were her natural daughter, and I have been truly blessed to have had her in my life.

It was strange to have two little boys sharing my bedroom! I had my single bed and the boys had bunk beds. Trisha's eldest, Leon, was very insecure like me, and often he would get into my bed and we would discuss our worries about there being a fire in the flat and would plan how we would get out. Neither of us could sleep without a light on in the hall outside of our bedroom. It was as if we were true brother and sister. I should have been a voice of reassurance – I was 13 and he was five – but I worried excessively about everything and so did he.

My youngest stepbrother, Gareth, was only two then, and was still very much the baby of the family, so growing up, we were not as close as me and Leon were at this time. Obviously, we could not continue to share a bedroom with me getting older, so it was decided that my dad and Trisha would buy a house in Watford. Those years are some of the happiest of my life. There were a lot of young people in the neighbourhood, and

I made a lot of friends whom I have stayed in contact with for the whole of my life.

I am wondering what they will think about me murdering Melissa and I hope that at least some of them will write and visit and that they will still love me. I made particularly good friends with the family opposite and eventually dated their son, Alan. Alan was my first true love. I have never loved in half measures. I adored him. Cheesy, I know, but I used to say that I could hear bells ring when we kissed! His parents were so lovely and kind to me and I adored his two sisters too. I genuinely felt like a member of their family.

Unfortunately, again, I loved Alan more than he loved me. On a night out I could see him chatting to another girl and I knew that they liked each other. I barely got any attention. He told me that he was just 'nipping to the loo' and the next thing I knew they left together and I had lost him. I was heartbroken. Not just for the fact that I was losing Alan, but also his whole family, whom I loved. This was rejection trigger number two and I honestly thought that I would never recover.

It made me behave irrationally and the ADHD kicked in big style. I did not know that I even had it then. I begged and pleaded with him to stay with me. I followed him to see what he was up to. I waited outside his work, lingering in the shadows, just so that I could see him. I once persuaded his father to drive me to the pub that they were frequenting and saw that they were laughing and playing pool. I threatened to ram the pool cue up her backside (but I was not as polite as that) and made myself look like a total psychopath. When I get like this, and the red mist fully descends, I do not stop to question myself or to worry about any consequences. In fact, when I get like this, I fear myself. Who knew that the playing of pool would end up being the bane of my life?

Fortunately, I did not lose all of Alan's family. I think that they honestly loved me and I have managed to keep them all in my life, until this time. Apart from my relationship with Alan, I was an outrageous flirt with all the boys and had a lot of boyfriends. I wasn't even sexually promiscuous, I just enjoyed the attention from boys. I guess that I was constantly looking for love and would settle for any that I could find. I had a very close relationship with my next-door-but-one neighbour, Robert, and we remain friends until this day. We may or may not have had some sort of dalliance, I will let you decide.

When I was 20, we moved from Watford to Devon. My dad and Trisha wanted to move out of the bustling city, so we went to live in the countryside where there was not a lot happening. I was sad to leave my friends and my life behind and felt very isolated. I was all set to move back to Watford, and even had a job lined up, and then I met Tom. My father was working as a milkman and so was Tom. Tom was hopeless with figures and, at that time, they had to keep their own written paperwork. So my father, ever the helpful work colleague, invited Tom around so that he could help him with his.

When I first met Tom, all I could say was that he was angry! He was the most sweary man I had ever encountered. He gave off the impression that he really did not give a shit and I liked it! Whatever drew me to that I will never know. I am surmising that because I had felt so repressed and hidden for the whole of my life, and that here was a person that was totally free to be himself, I admired it. It was the usual 'bad boy' story. He swore all the time, even the 'F-word', in front of his mum!

I mean he also wore winklepickers, and it was the '80s! He had longish hair, he wore braces – I mean, what there not to like? He said that he knew fairly quickly that he was going to marry me. So, we met in February, got engaged on his birthday in April and were married in October. It really was a whirlwind. There I went again, rushing headlong into something without ever really thinking about the consequences.

I am not going to go into too much detail about my first marriage here. My children might read this one day and I would not want to hurt Tom, or them, or his mother, whom I love. Our marriage had some extremely happy times and some not so. But I am pleased for him that he has now moved on, has remarried, and has had two further children. I do hope that one day we can be friends, but even if that never happens, I will be forever grateful that he has given me two wonderful children, so I am glad that some lasting good came out of our marriage.

***

This brings me on to my subsequent marriage to Frank. I thought that when I met Frank that he and Tom were completely different. Frank was more serious and pensive and he certainly would not have dreamt of swearing in front of his mum! He did not wear his heart on his sleeve like Tom did. I often knew what Tom was thinking before he said it. But Frank, well, he was much more difficult to read. He was very critical of other people and their faults, including mine. He only gave me a four-out-of-five in the looks department, which any woman would tell you is a big no-no, even if you think it! If nothing else, I must have felt that he was at least extremely honest.

He was very dogmatic in his views and beliefs, but he was not in touch with his emotions. His first wife, Sharon, had even warned me that he had no emotions! So – and you know the cut of my jib by now – another red flag presented itself to me and I totally ignored it and for whatever reason thought that it would be a good idea to marry him and then expected it all to end well! It was not too far into our relationship that I suspected that he was on the autism spectrum. I had worked for many years with children with autism and I recognised the signs.

He was an extremely clever and bright man. That is one of the things that attracted me to him. He was very analytical and good at problem solving. This meant that any or all household tasks could be done much more strategically and efficiently by him than by me. I am haphazard at best and have no methodology in anything. This meant that I chucked stuff into the dishwasher with gay abandon and he would come along and organize everything so that it not only looked 'neat' but also so that you could fit much more in.

When we went shopping together, he would 'group' items into the right area of the shopping trolley, stacked perfectly, of course, and then at the end he would pack the shopping into bags more tidily than I would have thought possible. So good was he that he could have had a job packing people's shopping in Harrods. If I went shopping on my own, it was every man – or tin of beans – for himself. The bread might be squashed, by the time I got home, or the milk might have leaked everywhere, but I continued to throw it in and hope for the best.

At night time, when I get undressed, I fling my clothes on the floor (I do not think it matters, as I am the one who must pick them up), whereas he would have folded his and put them on his chair, even getting clean socks out for the following morning and then going downstairs to prepare everything that he would need to use before going to work for the following morning. As irritating as it could be, and so completely opposite to my way of doing things, I loved all of this about him.

We really could not be more different, personality-wise. He is quiet and shy. I am shy, but try to cover it with being extrovert. I have a lot of friends and love socialising. Frank just liked it to be me and him. On our own. Period. I must add that he was quite happy for me to go out with my friends, but he would stay at home and do something alone. He had no friends. He always said to me that he did not like or want friends and that I was his only friend. This was a massive reassurance to me, as it meant that he was never going to leave me and that he *needed* me. I did not think that this would ever change, that is, until *she* came along and ruined everything.

Chapter 6

For the first eight years of our marriage, I can honestly say that I had never been happier. As much as Frank felt that I was his best friend, he was also mine. I leaned on him heavily for support and I found his support to be unwavering. I was reliant on him for everything. This amuses me now, as people think that I am strong and brave by the outward demeanour that I portray. I might seem confident, but this has not always been the case and most often I am floundering emotionally, without a great deal to anchor me. You may have heard of the four different personality types? Secure, anxious, avoidant, and fearful. I suppose we are all a combination of each of them, but I thought that Frank at least was secure and was exactly what I needed, as I am anxious.

In July of 2012, I found a lump in my breast. I had a sixth sense that it was not going to be good news. My intuition has been a valuable tool in my life, as often I can tell what is going to happen before it does. I do not know if it is divine, but it has made me a realist. So, I was not overly shocked when I had to collect the test results at the hospital and was told that I had cancer. Even though I knew it was coming, you can never be fully prepared to hear those words. Frank was with me when I went for my results, and he significantly paled in colour and looked visibly upset. From that moment, it now transpires that something in him 'died' as far as his love for me was concerned. But I was not to know this, or even be told this, for a further ten years.

***

Frank's family do not manage unwelcome news very well, preferring instead to 'not think about it and it will go away'. But this was a very real life-confronting diagnosis and, on reflection, I do not think that Frank could deal with it. My consultant said that my cancer was Stage 3, was aggressive, and said that I would need rigorous treatment to manage it. I do not suppose that I will ever know now, but did Frank think that I was going to die, so emotionally cut himself off from me? I hope that is the case, because the alternative means that he never really loved me at all and that is too painful for me to even think about. But like I have told you, at times, he did not show any emotion and I do not have a clue to this day what he thought about this new life situation.

And so it began. An entire year of treatment. Starting with two operations to remove the tumour and then the tissue around it. The surgeon then tried to construct a new breast out of what was left. My nipple was removed and then sewn back on again. Vigorous and unpleasant courses of chemotherapy and radiotherapy then ensued. All my body hair fell out. Frank did seem very distressed about this. I will not forget his face when my hairdresser shaved off the remaining strands of hair from my head. It was impossible to hide from this and pretend that everything was as it had been.

It must be a stark realisation, seeing your wife, now hairless, and looking ill. How can you bury your head and pretend that this is not happening? Your wife, who was usually very active, is now also lying around feeling ill and tired all the time, because of the drugs, and you are observing first-hand her new and weird eating habits as she finds that all food tastes vile and she is constantly feeling nauseous.

I was hurt that Frank did not come with me for any of my appointments, but was it too much for him? This reads like I am trying to protect him from taking any sort of responsibility, but I am purely just trying to understand it. At home, he tried to take care of me and cooked food that I fancied, so he did try to help me. I know that he did not like hospitals, but who does? My views on this are absolute. It is tough, but go in – not for you, but for the person that is ill!

During my treatment we did try to make love, but it just did not happen. Frank was totally turned off. Firstly, through my lack of hair, and during the chemotherapy treatment he said that kissing me was like sticking his tongue into a jar of raw liver. Granted, that sounds unpleasant, and I do understand, but I really needed him at this time, and I wanted at least something in my life to be normal. I was facing the possibility that this disease might kill me. I was not afraid of dying, as I believe that there is something beyond this world, but I was not ready to go just yet, and I still adored him with the whole of my being.

Once my treatment was complete, there was a collective feeling of relief on both our parts. My hair grew back, albeit different. I had chestnut brown hair pre-cancer and now my hair was grey, so I did what any self-respecting vain person would do and went blonde. I have been dyeing my hair blonde ever since. Did Frank not like blondes? Was I too different? Also, I *had* changed. I was very insecure about my appearance now; my breast was deformed, and I had put on weight due to the steroids and the hormone drugs I was put on. We both really needed some counselling, but Frank is not the sort of person to talk about how he is feeling. He had no friends to talk to and he would never have confided in his family. I was so blessed in comparison; my friends were amazing and supported me throughout, but I had nobody that I could talk to about our lack of intimacy, as I did not want to be disloyal to Frank.

After this, we tried to get on with our lives, but I missed our physical intimacy terribly. I was in such deep and emotional pain, that I cannot find the words to even describe it. Even saying that it was like a bereavement does not really come close. As a person who needs a plenty of touching and cuddles, it really hurt when Frank became wary of showing me too much affection in case I thought that it might culminate in our having sex. So he withdrew, physically and mentally. I cannot describe strongly enough how rejected and unattractive this made me feel. I was also starting to go through the menopause, as the hormone drugs pushed me into an early menopause. I was only 45 when it was discovered that I had breast cancer and I am not going to lie – the menopause for me has been absolute hell.

Already slightly mentally unstable and suffering with ADHD, I now had to negotiate living with hot flushes that were so bad I could not even apply make-up without it running off my face. I had night sweats that caused me to be wringing-wet in the middle of the night. My hair used to stick to the back of my neck with the sweat and rivulets of perspiration used to run between my breasts and down my back and then I would be freezing cold. I suddenly became claustrophobic and even being in the shower used to make me feel too enclosed, so part way through washing I had to open the door, just to feel free and to breathe. Emotionally, I was a mess. My poor children had to deal with me crying a lot, and I knew that at times I was being unreasonable but did not know how to stop. I can fully understand how some menopausal women go completely crazy. I also had terrible brain fog; I could not concentrate or remember things and did loopy things like put the teabags in the fridge.

All of this knocked my confidence for six. I developed anxiety, particularly in shops. I could no longer get on a bus, or deal with too many people. Frank did not understand. I was a different person and none of it was good. Also, he did not want to have sex with me. I used to sob and plead and beg him to get some help. He would just declare, "Sorry, it doesn't work," whilst wagging his flaccid penis at me and shrugging. Please remember at the beginning of this what I told you about our sex life. We were the embodiment of the *Kama Sutra*. I missed him and missed 'us' terribly. I have felt unloved before, but this was on a new level. I could not understand it; surely if he loved me he would have tried to do something about it.

Chapter 7

Obviously Frank and I could not spend the whole of our marriage having sex, as much as I would have liked to. However, I did not expect to have a sexless marriage from the age of 45 onwards. And I will admit that I was more than a little resentful. I really needed someone to confide in, but due to my loyalty to Frank, I did not tell anybody. I almost phoned my cancer nurse, I almost phoned Macmillan. I joined support groups of those that had breast cancer and anonymously shared what had happened with people I did not know, and who really could not help me. And then one day, I cracked.

I was feeling particularly lonely and unloved. Frank and I had previously had another one of our 'sex talks' and during the conversation he said, "Who is to say if I were to meet somebody else then it might start to work again?" Well, this broke me. I was absolutely devastated. Of course, he backtracked and said, "But I am not planning on meeting anybody else, so it will be fine." This should have rung massive alarm bells, but again, I was so sure of his love for me that I did not ever think that it could happen. The next day when Trisha visited, I lost it. I broke down and confessed my big secret. It was a genuine relief to tell someone. Though I still felt guilty for betraying my husband.

I have learned, though, that many women do not actually enjoy sex. So many would look upon my predicament as a blessing! But, again, you need to remember, what it was like beforehand and what I had lost. I also confided in my 'bosom buddy', Elaine. I had met Elaine and Ann during a course that we all did during our cancer treatments. Elaine was a massive support to me and I knew that I needed to look at this all differently if I were going to survive. I loved Frank with my whole heart, and I had to decide whether I could live within a sexless marriage with Frank, or be without him. And in the end, there was no competition, so I chose Frank. And I remained faithful and upheld my marriage vows until the end.

***

I tried my hardest not to feel resentful, or to get too upset about our lack of intimacy and decided that I would not put too much pressure on Frank. But a few months later I went to the doctor and hoped that she would at least offer me help and support, but she was very dismissive (another woman who did not enjoy sex then?). I broke down and she passed me a box of tissues. She did say that she could prescribe Frank some Viagra, but for that he would need to go in and see her himself. This was not a conversation that I was looking forward to having when I got home.

After much persuasion and angst on both our parts, Frank did eventually go to the GP and got some Viagra, but I do not think he was happy about it. He resented me for putting him under pressure but I still felt that if he cared about me enough, he would want to sort it out, which clearly he did not. We tried the Viagra a handful of times. It made Frank have a blinding headache that took him a while to recover from and it created 'sex by appointment', which is not my bag. One must take it an hour beforehand and by then my libido, at least, had completely expired. It did not work for us, so in the end, I admitted defeat.

So, our roles completely changed. We were no longer husband and wife, we were 'house-sharing'. I am sure many couples manage perfectly well with this arrangement and, indeed, I did honestly think that Frank was my best friend and so we rubbed along nicely as teammates. We never argued, we did get along extremely well, and I genuinely felt happy and content. I really dislike conflict and was grateful that, if nothing else, that we had a peaceful coexistence. He seemed happy in his own world with me on the periphery – he partaking in his hobby of woodturning, at which he was extremely proficient. All self-taught, a true savant. While I, who love to socialise and meeting up with friends, did my own thing. But, at the end of the day, I always went home to Frank, who was my security, and to our house that we had created together.

Like I said, Frank did not like mixing with other people. If there was a function or a party that we needed to go to, there was a standing joke between us. He would say, "What time can we leave?" or "How long will we have to stay?" I would then give him a time that I felt was appropriate that would not be too much time for him and would not appear to be too rude for the hosts. Sometimes, Frank would not be in the right mood to socialise at all, be it us visiting people or people dropping in to see us. You could see by his face that he was miserable and not enjoying himself, which would make me inwardly cringe and I would excuse his behaviour, by saying that he was 'tired' or 'had a bad day'. I was always trying to make light of it and when he was not being social with people, I would try to talk too much, to make up for it. Sometimes, it was exhausting, but I did put his lack of social skills and tact (he had none) down to his Asperger's Syndrome.

The only person Frank had a genuine relationship with, besides me, was my daughter, Rosie. They had a strong connection and a mutual respect, even though Rosie could be difficult and headstrong and Frank could be super critical – to the point where they drove each other quite mad. But after their argument, they would make up and he was surprisingly affectionate with her. He also had a strong affinity with two of our cats (we had three). Ginge, who we got first, was his feline best friend. He used to hold her up in the air and tell her how much he loved her, and they would play fight and she would run out to greet him when he came home from work. And then again with our youngest cat, Tiny, who slept on his side of the bed every night.

You can feel jealous of a cat, you know…

***

So, we continued in a state of contentment, never arguing, being good friends and companions. Admittedly, our lives might have seemed a little dull to others. It consisted of us both working, he as a taxi driver then, and me as a passenger assistant, taking children with special needs, to and from school in a minibus. It was my idea that Frank should switch careers from driving a lorry, to being a taxi driver. When he first started doing it, it paid extremely well and appeared to be a desirable choice, but I should have known better. My father's last job before he died was also working as a taxi driver and he had an affair with one of his clients. My poor stepmother really did not deserve this and most taxi drivers I have met since seem to have real trouble keeping it in their trousers! What other job is there, where you can go off grid, be out all the hours God sends and where you are able to turn off your location? When I told Trisha that Frank was going to be a taxi driver, she was suitably appalled, but I said, "Do not worry, Frank would never do that to me."

I know – I am the most gullible person I have ever known and am stupid with a capital 'S'.

When we both got home from work, we would have our evening meal, usually with the plate on our laps, watching *The Chase*. We were hardly going to set the world on fire, but I had previously had enough drama in my life and enjoyed the quiet tranquillity of how things were. If only Frank had told me that he was bored. There are so many 'if onlys', but I loved him so much and so unconditionally; I was genuinely happy with my lot. I did at times feel terribly lonely, but that was mainly caused by the lack of intimacy and affection. Things became much harder for me emotionally when the children moved out. Firstly, when my son, James, moved to London to go to university and then when Rosie moved out to live with her boyfriend. Frank, like most men, was overjoyed when the children moved out, but I was heartbroken and had an unbelievably bad case of 'empty nest syndrome'. You see, my children mean the absolute world to me.

Chapter 8

So, Frank and I bumbled along like this for some time, and I still never doubted his love for me. My son, James, had met Sofia at the University of East London and they were very much in love. After university, they lived for a while in London before coming back to live with us. It was so lovely to have them home, so my 'empty nest syndrome' was healed, or at least delayed, until another time. They became engaged, were in the process of trying to buy a house and were trying to organise their wedding, when the world was hit with the Covid-19 Coronavirus pandemic.

Obviously, this was unprecedented in our lifetime. I personally did not feel that afraid. Having already faced death with cancer, I was in a better position than most. The only thing I felt dreadful about was the effect that this might have on our children, and I felt it was so unfair for them having to live in such uncertain times (poor James and Sofia tried to organise their wedding six times before they were married). My daughter, Rosie, was a nurse, so worked throughout the whole thing, even though I knew she was frightened. She told me that she had seen experienced doctors openly weeping, with the situation being so demanding and traumatic. Poor Rosie also lost a work colleague who took her own life due to the pressure, and she was only 22. I am so proud that Rosie got through this difficult period in her life, mostly unscathed.

Mine and my mother's relationship was difficult throughout most of my life. This was not helped by her gradually becoming dependant on alcohol in her later years. But it was still a huge shock to get a phone call from my sister, Fern, to say that she had collapsed during a barbecue that they were having and that my mother had been taken to hospital in an ambulance. It was 'touch and go' all day and I had one of my intuitions that this was not going to end well. It transpired that she had suffered a massive heart attack and we three remaining children (we had previously and devastatingly lost our sister, Joy, to a drug overdose) had to make the decision to have her life support turned off, as, otherwise, we had been informed there was a strong possibility that she would have lived the rest of her life in a vegetative state.

I was grief-stricken. I was sorrowful that we did not have a better relationship. I was heartbroken that it was now too late to forge a better relationship and I was terribly sad for her, as her life had not been easy. My feelings were confused too. Two weeks before she died we had a huge argument; we had not even been talking properly to each other when she died. I loved her and yet I was still cross with her. I really did not know what to do with myself. It has taken me three years to fully come to terms with everything and to properly forgive her. I have found personally that it is harder to deal with the death of a loved one if your relationship had been troubled. There are too many 'what-ifs'.

We were not allowed to mix with other people, so this meant that we could not see Frank's children, Tilly and Bradley. I found that difficult, and not seeing Rosie, too, was very hard. I was signed off work as I was classed as 'vulnerable' and, of course, Frank could not do any taxi driving. 2020 was a strange year! The four of us mostly spent time in the garden, as it was glorious weather. It was like this tragedy had befallen all humans, but the weather gods had decided to make it up to us, with a dry, sweltering summer. I did not notice at the time, but James and Sofia have told me since that they had noticed Frank's drinking had become quite excessive.

I know that during the pandemic most people's drinking, and eating, had become somewhat excessive, not excluding my own, but Frank had always enjoyed a bit more alcohol than most, so I failed to notice the elevation in his drinking habits. I do not know if this has been a contributory factor into what happened with us. I will let you decide. I do know from my own experience with an alcoholic mother that alcohol can completely take over somebody's life and can change their personality beyond all recognition. Certainly, Frank was about to become a person that I did not recognise anymore.

***

At some point, during the national lockdown that the government had imposed, key workers were allowed to return to work and the children of keyworkers could also return to school. Just before this happened, Frank was approached by a local taxi operator who offered him a contract to take a child to school. This job came with two passenger assistants who shared the job. Frank had done school runs before, so I was not at all concerned about him working with two women even though he would be spending several hours a week with each of them. It never crossed my mind that this was about to cause the absolute and final death knell on our marriage.

Frank went back to work before I did, so I decided to use my free time to completely redecorate the house. It did not escape my notice that Frank started to spend a lot of time talking about Daisy. Daisy was the younger of his two passenger assistants, being only 20 years old. She was also the daughter of Keith, who had offered Frank the school run in the first place, so Keith was effectively his boss. I had been contemplating painting my kitchen cupboards and Daisy had painted hers, so the first time I met her was when Frank took me around to her flat to have a look.

She took a while to answer the front door. When she eventually opened it, she looked tearful and dishevelled, having just had a massive row with her dad. She was quite a bit taller than me, was very slim and had long blonde hair, though it was tied up on this occasion. She showed me her cupboard doors and I was impressed. Frank was concerned that she seemed upset and was truly kind and comforted her with words of praise and kindness. I know what you are thinking. *No red flags? You complete fool.* I was proud of him for being so supportive to a young, vulnerable girl. When will I ever learn?

I liked Daisy. She had a very bubbly personality, and she was quite confident and funny. She had a second job as a bartender in our local Conservative club, separate from her school run with Frank, and she was immensely popular among the clientele. Certainly, Frank liked her a lot. He talked about her frequently and would have done anything to help her. He also felt sorry for her, due to her relationship with her parents being quite volatile. The next time I met her she turned up on our doorstep, upset again, after another argument with her parents.

I felt very tender towards her and tried to show her kindness, because of the difficulties I had with my own mother. Before long, Daisy was a regular visitor to our house and, at first, I did not mind at all. This happened just after James and Sofia bought a house in the north of England and had moved out for good. Rosie had also moved out and moved in with her boyfriend, Danny, so I was upset and lonely and still grieving for my mum. I felt that I had been given Daisy to love and care for like a daughter to distract my mind from the emotional pain I was in.

As time progressed, Frank and Daisy spent more time together, and not just while doing the school run. Often, while I was painting or sanding wood, I would hear them laughing and joking around. Well, anybody who knew Frank would not have recognised this new man! Ordinarily, he was quite miserable, not one for having a joke, or even laughing. I began to get feelings of jealousy. I did try to control them, I really did; she was a vulnerable child. Surely, she could not be interested in Frank in a sexual way, could she? Or, for the same reason, he, her?

Daisy spent increased time at our house. My daughter, Rosie, was now also having feelings of jealousy. Rosie was round one morning when Frank and Daisy got home from their run with drinks and burgers from McDonald's and were laughing when they came in to the house. Frank was infamous for his meanness and now he was 'treating' someone else to a McDonald's! Rosie and I were both upset. When Daisy left, we told Frank what we thought, but I do not think he understood how hurt we felt.

Soon Daisy started arriving unannounced at our house – Frank just kept inviting her over. She would be there when I got home from my own school run in the morning and again in the afternoon. Frank started asking me if Daisy could stay for dinner, which she often did. I began to feel resentment, but I was also having inner turmoil. This poor girl needed us and I have always aimed to be a kind and loving person. I was having constant battles in my mind about doing the right thing. Rosie found out that Daisy was staying for meals and she resented her too for having free meals, when she had to pay rent when she lived at home. I tried to state a good case as to why we were being kind to Daisy, whilst also beginning to despair myself at the amount of the time she was spending with us.

I felt used. I was doing the decorating single-handedly whilst also cooking meals for the two of them. Daisy did not help with the dishes. I was working hard, whilst they were laughing. They both smoked and they would have a cigarette together. She would sit on my seat on the sofa, next to him, while I sat on the other sofa alone. When we went shopping, Frank, who was previously so careful with money and our spending, would buy her ciders. As I am telling you all of this, I am feeling increasingly naïve and stupid!

Daisy then started to come round every evening, and at weekends. Frank and I had started going for walks to increase our fitness, and quite often Daisy would come with us. It was starting to become about just the two of them, with me tagging along. The most difficult aspect of all of this was that I had grown to love her like an extra daughter and I really did like her as a person, I just wished that Frank would have noticed my existence, despite his newfound friendship.

The term 'gaslighting' seems to be a modern term that is bandied around all too often, but reflecting on this challenging time, it was happening to me, and daily. I would ask Frank nicely if we could spend some time alone, stating clearly that I loved Daisy, but that I was finding it too much. He would then berate me for being unkind to a vulnerable girl who needed our help, thus making me fell terribly guilty and that I was a nasty person. I do blame myself for allowing this situation to spiral out of control and since I have 'come out', all females that I have spoken to have said that they would not have allowed this to happen right at the beginning and have said that of course no woman would like their husband having such a close relationship with a much younger attractive woman! Again, all I can say is that I trusted Frank implicitly.

Chapter 9

Over time, the situation at home was becoming intolerable. I spent a lot of time in tears and the whole situation was making me ill. I loved Daisy, but wanted my marriage back to normal. I pleaded with Frank to at least stop Daisy coming around so frequently, but then he would make me feel awful by saying that the problem was with me because I didn't like him having any friends. Remember that, up until this point, he had no friends and had said that I was his only friend!

It simply is not true that I did not want him to have any friends. But was it 'normal' for him to want to have a female friend that was only 20 years old? I used to feel sorry for him that he did not have any friends. I have many, and they have been like a lifeline to me throughout my life. I actively encouraged him to go to his school reunion in the hope that he would rekindle some friendships with his old school friends and he had not really wanted to go. So it hurt that now he accused me of not wanting him to have any friends, as nothing could be further from the truth.

But Daisy, for some reason, was different. He admired her bubbly and confident personality. Perhaps it reminded him of how I used to be pre-cancer. One of the incidents that sticks out in my mind was when I came downstairs one day and he had his finger up her nose, helping her do up her nose ring! I do not know if that seems intimate to you, but I personally found it to be so, and we had an argument when she left.

He then told me that I was crazy, had gone mad and that the menopause had made me mental.

I certainly felt as if my mental health was deteriorating. I had a feeling of unease and unrest all the time. Because Frank drilled it into me that the problem lay with me and my vivid imagination, I did not share any of what was going on with anybody else. I also felt so bad, that there was this poor girl that I should be being kind to and helping, and now I was being 'nasty' and 'very unchristian'. It was such a difficult position to be in. It was around this time that I tried to seek some help for my menopausal symptoms, as I thought it must be me. I even convinced myself that I was being unreasonable.

Because I have had breast cancer and it is hormone-receptive, I was not supposed to take HRT or anything with oestrogen in it, so my only choice was to go down other avenues of medical help. My stepmum, Trisha, offered to pay for some oestrogen cream for me over the internet that you apply to your wrist and that is absorbed into your skin. I felt bad doing this – was it dangerous? I drafted an email to the manufacturers explaining my condition and they said that it was perfectly safe to use, but I guess they would, wouldn't they?

But as much as I applied this religiously to my wrist and tried to remain 'quiet and good' (which is my thing, remember, so as not to not upset the equilibrium), Frank continued to invite Daisy into our home all the time. And however upset I got, he made it clear that his friendship with Daisy was more important than anything. More even, than his relationship with me. I then started to wonder – I know, I am a bit slow – if he had begun to develop sexual feelings for her. I would tell you now, after much thought about the situation, that I think Frank meeting

Daisy reinvigorated his sexual urges. I do not think, however, that this was reciprocated and I do think that Daisy truly only looked upon Frank as a father figure.

I was quite alarmed when I sorted through our coats on our coat rack one day and a shiny pebble (heart-shaped) fell out of Frank's coat pocket. When he came from work, I asked him why there was a pebble in his pocket, and he went very dreamy-eyed and said, "Oh, Daisy gave it to me while we were at the beach." I knew that they used to stop off at the beach on their way to the school for a cigarette break, but I found the fact that he had kept this pebble very weird.

I did not feel able to talk to anybody about this situation, as, by now, Frank had totally convinced me that all my fears were in my head and that my behaviour was irrational. This 'gaslighting', although I did not know then that this is what it was, went along the lines of a dialogue that went something like this.

Me: "I love Daisy as much as you do, but I am tired of seeing her every day and I miss the fact that we no longer spend any time together on our own."

Frank: "I cannot believe you are being so selfish! She is my friend and I want to help her."

Me: "I have not asked you not to help her and I am willing to help her too, I would just like to spend some time together on our own."

Frank: "You have never liked me having friends. It is OK for you to have friends, but I am not allowed to have any!

"Me: "I have never asked you to not have any friends, but Daisy is a 20-year-old girl and your boss's daughter."

Frank: "Now you are just being unkind. What is wrong with you?"

And so it went on, for week after week. Frank made it truly clear that I was no longer of any significance to him and that Daisy was his soul focus. It reminded me of the scene in the film *American Beauty* when Kevin Spacey's character fell in love with his daughter's friend and imagined her naked in a bath of rose petals!

***

This was when Frank started to be secretive with his phone. He went from leaving it in the house to taking it everywhere he went. It used to drive me potty when he used to leave it in the house and then go out and do woodturning in his workshop and then people would phone to speak to him and I would have to run out and give him his phone. I used to plead with him to take it outside with him and he never would. Until now. Now it went everywhere that he went. He was constantly texting and reading texts, sometimes he would put his phone on silent. When I questioned it, he went back to me being 'crazy', 'mad' and 'menopausal'. "Why do you have such a suspicious and paranoid mind?"

Things then took a very bizarre turn. Since the menopause, I have been an exceptionally light sleeper, so, I would wake up in the night and realise that Frank was not in bed. I would go downstairs and he would be sitting at the dining table in the early hours, drinking vodka or Jack Daniels and chain-smoking.

He looked awful. This went on for weeks. I would sit with him and try to coax out of him what was going on. He would just say that he was stressed. Of course, the phone stayed with him. He would think nothing of drinking two thirds of a bottle of spirits every day. This is when his drinking became fully out of his control. When I said I was concerned about the smoking and drinking, he would get really cross with me and complain about my nagging.

Having had an alcoholic mother, I was genuinely scared for him. I know how this story ends, and it is never pretty. After several weeks of him doing this and me almost tearing my hair out, he confessed the reason for his behaviour. Daisy was on drugs! This seems wrong, but I felt as if a massive weight had lifted off my shoulders! Everything now made sense. This is why he had been trying to help her. He was sitting up at night, in case she overdosed and needed him.

I have told you that I am stupid, but I thought that now he had shared this massive weight, we could get back to normal. It turned out that Daisy was doing cocaine and ketamine, to name but two. I told him that him sitting up all night drinking and smoking was not going to save Daisy, as these people can only be helped once they realise themselves that they have a problem. I told him to tell her dad, but he would not, and I was not permitted to tell her that I knew, as she had sworn him to secrecy.

This secret that he had held back from me had nearly destroyed our relationship. I hoped that, now he had shared, there would not be any further secrets between us. But still the drinking continued apace and then we would argue about that. I thought he would end up losing his job, as every morning he must have been over the limit when he was doing his school run and he was taking a vulnerable child to school who had special needs. Had Frank now become an alcoholic and was it too late to save him from himself?

Daisy was very much into fashion and Frank, who had never been into fashion *at all*, now started to care about his appearance. He started to buy clothes, hoodies and trainers that were 'named'! It was like I was watching someone that I thought I knew, inside and out, completely change before my very eyes. He would ask for Daisy's opinion on his new clothes. I was watching him have a midlife crisis. Daisy then suggested to him that he join our local Conservative club, where she had her second job, and I was amazed when he told me that he thought this was a clever idea. Again, I had a dreadful feeling of unease and disquiet in my soul about what was going to happen when he did. As it was to transpire, I was not mad at all; again my intuition was going to prove to be correct.

He went to join the Conservative club with Melissa and her husband, Nick. Melissa being his other work colleague. He had now stopped mentioning Daisy quite as much and now started talking incessantly about them instead. I was amazed again that he went through with joining a club! He had always hated going out and socialising. Remember, he used to ask when we could leave a social gathering. What was going on? I was genuinely perplexed. In the background, I was feeling increasingly anxious. I could sense that things were going to change for us, and not for the better.

Frank tried to persuade me that joining the club would be better for 'us'. That we could go out as a foursome with Melissa and Nick, that they enjoyed playing pool and he really used to enjoy it in his youth. He started to become animated when he talked about them. Usually, Frank did not get animated about anything! He told me that they were a really nice couple and how much he liked Nick in particular. Yes, he could see the pair of them being friends! He also said that Melissa and I would 'get on' and that we had a lot in common as we had both had previously had breast cancer. Melissa and I could not be more different as it turns out.

Chapter 10

I was first introduced to Melissa, albeit briefly, when Frank and I returned with shopping for our friends, Patrick and Diana. We did a twice weekly shop for them throughout the restrictions during the pandemic, as they looked after their vulnerable grandson. They lived next-door-but-one from Melissa and Nick and we would spend some time on the doorstep talking to them after our shop. On this occasion, Frank spent our usual chat time talking to Melissa on her doorstep. He briefly introduced us to each other, and we both waved.

The next time I met her, we went round to their house as my friend, Linda, wanted some tadpoles and Frank had told me that Melissa had thousands of them and had said that I could collect some of the surplus from her pond to take to Linda's. Frank would claim at a later date that I disliked Melissa on sight. That simply is not true, I did not even know her at this point and I always give people a chance. She and Nick seemed genuinely nice. I am not going to lie though; I did find the fact that Melissa was not wearing a bra a bit disconcerting, especially as she was a bit older and her breasts were hardly 'perky'.

So, of course, when we got home, I asked Frank if he fancied Melissa, and he told me not to be so ridiculous! He asked if I had I seen the warts on her face. "She is not much to look at, and most of all, she is married to my friend, Nick. First, you were jealous of Daisy and now you are jealous of Melissa. What is wrong with you!" Even at this point I felt vulnerable, like the foundations of my life were starting to shake. I cannot explain this to you, but I had a really deep feeling in my gut that my life was soon going to implode, but I did not know how or why.

I have already explained to you how bad I felt about myself after breast cancer. I felt *so* unattractive. I had put on weight because of the drugs I had been on, my hair was dry and brittle after the chemotherapy and was falling out. One of my breasts was now deformed after two surgeries, but the worst of all these things, and superseding all the others, was the fact that my husband no longer found me desirable nor wanted to have any intimacy with me. I cannot express enough the enormity of pain that I felt because of this, it went right to the core of my very soul.

Frank's intimate relationship with Daisy had not helped the situation. How could I compete with a tall, slim, blonde 'girl' that displayed the confidence of youth? I quickly discovered that Frank had been talking to Melissa about my insecurities and the fact that we had been having disagreements about Daisy. In fact, as I was soon to discover, Frank talked to Melissa about *everything* that went on in our home and in our lives, without any sense of loyalty or of shame.

The night Frank first suggested that the four of us went to the Conservative club, I was wracked with nerves and I felt sick. I spent ages trying on clothes and wondering what to wear, I had not even properly got to know Melissa yet, but as Frank talked about her all the time, she, and he, already made me feel inferior. I know that this sounds a bit bonkers. Frank did not even try to make me feel better, he just ridiculed me for my nerves and berated me for not wanting to go out with them. My self-esteem, at this point, was on the floor.

When we turned up, Melissa and Nick were already there. Melissa told me that she was nervous about meeting me! What had Frank said to her? She had very dark, almost jet-black long hair that fell loosely over her shoulders. It had a tousled look, like it had not been brushed properly. It only added to her allure. It was like she was so busy being sexy that she did not have time for personal hygiene. I imagined that she released top-of-the-range pheromones that overtook any need for washing. Every time that I met her, she looked like she had just got up after having a night of vigorous sex.

I wondered then, as I wonder now, if she had been of Romany descent. Her eyes were dark brown and her skin was olive and smooth. She walked around confidently like she was ready to conquer the world; just a flick of her hair, here and there, so that all the men knew that she was confident in the bedroom. She had long slender fingers. There was no need for nail varnish; she had no time for women who tried to make themselves more attractive to men. This came easily to her, and she, above everyone, loved herself the most. No need for any make-up either then, apart from lip gloss, showing that minimal effort was required and that she was 'good to go'. One time I looked down at her feet and noticed that she had dirt under her toenails, I speculated that she had just had sex in a flowerbed.

She was also quite masculine, both in her attitude and in her appearance. She was not at all a girly-girl. I could not, for example, imagine her wearing a flowery frock or heels – that would be way too feminine for her. And she behaved like 'one of the lads' enjoying the company of men much more than that of women. She was quite hard-faced in temperament and not at all emotional. Is this what men really want? Because

I am the most emotional person ever and maybe that is why my luck with men has been lower than zero.

Melissa's husband, Nick, had silvery-grey hair and a matching beard. He looked like a distinguished silver fox. He was much better looking than he thought he was. And had a much softer personality than Melissa. A quietly spoken man, with not a great deal of confidence. His features were quite 'rugged', but not as rugged as Frank's. I always said that Frank's complexion was quite weather-beaten or joked that he had had a hard paper-round. He had a similar build to Frank, both having a little bit of middle-aged spread.

Nick was a taxi driver, like Frank, and so spent a lot of time out of the house. It is quite unbelievable, but true, that Nick had fancied Melissa since they were at school together and that he waited for her for his whole life, whilst she had three previous marriages, the last one being with Nick's best friend, whom she ended up leaving so that she could be with Nick. She also came with 'baggage' having a son and a daughter by one of the husbands (I am not sure which one). She had a son slightly older than my son, James, called David, whom she hardly saw as he lived abroad, and a daughter around my son's age called Justine who lived just down the road. Even then, she did not see a great deal of her daughter either. Melissa was not at all maternal.

I could not then, and certainly cannot now, comprehend what Nick could see in Melissa. I wish that he had more confidence in himself and what he had to offer. I think that Melissa could sense this – she would have had to be blind not to – and therefore his devotion added to her own sense of self-importance. I have never seen, before or since, a man look at a woman with as much love as I saw from Nick when he looked at her. He was clearly totally besotted and looked at her like she was an angel that had just dropped off a cloud. Melissa was certainly *his* love of his life. Her cruelty, which came later, to such a nice man still sickens me to this day.

It was such a pity that she did not treat Nick with more respect. He was a good man, who did not deserve what they did to him. My anger on Nick's behalf is still palpable. When I beat Melissa to death with that piece of wood, I did not just do it for me. I have always had a keen sense of justice and I will always stand up for the underdog. No, I did if for Nick too and he is very welcome. I hope that if you are reading this, Nick, or that when you get to hear about what I did, that you will feel at least a little bit pleased. She cannot hurt you now, or any other man. I hope that, moving forward, you will find a nice woman who will appreciate your gentle spirit and that these events have made you a better judge of character.

***

Back to our first date as a foursome. So, we were in the Conservative club, and I went to the loo and was closely followed by Melissa. I was wearing a grey fitted polka dot dress, which must have been about the 20th outfit that I had tried on, until I felt happy (ish). As I came out of the cubicle, Melissa exclaimed in a slightly raised voice, whilst standing aside to appraise me like I was an exhibit at the zoo or something, "I do not know what you think is wrong with you! I mean, you look all right, and you don't look fat!" Well, I was utterly dumbfounded! This meant that Frank had told Melissa about all my insecurities and now she was using them against me! I do not know how I managed to hold it together – this was a back-handed compliment if ever I had heard one. I looked 'all right'? Well thank you, that's OK then. This was to be the first of many times that Melissa would persecute me and where Frank would back her and not me.

I told Frank later that night what had happened in the toilets and he really couldn't comprehend that she had done anything wrong. He could not see that Melissa drawing attention to my appearance had made me feel a hundred times worse. Also, I was upset that he had felt it necessary to discuss my personal business with her. This was not the Frank that I knew. The Frank that I knew was a very private person and, I thought, very loyal. He was gradually disappearing before my very eyes.

Our seeing Melissa and Nick became increasingly frequent. At first, I did try to be polite and friendly. One sunny afternoon, Frank invited them into our garden for drinks and I asked Melissa why they had moved from their old home to their current one, which was a five-minute walk from our house. She proceeded to tell me that she had 'persuaded' her dad to sell his house and that they had now moved into this big, detached house around the corner. She intimated that her dad probably had not 'got long left', so at some point, the house would become hers and Nick's. I found this distasteful and, by now, I was not liking what I was seeing or hearing.

During the lockdown restrictions, Frank had turned the summerhouse in our garden into a bar, which meant more drinking and more socialising. By the time we had seen first Daisy, and then Melissa and Nick so regularly, we hardly had any time left just for the two of us. Our arguing about Daisy had now escalated onto arguing about the amount of time that

Frank wanted to spend with Melissa and Nick. It was like he was totally obsessed with them. At first, I tried to put this down to his Asperger's Syndrome and tried to make allowances. Having worked with children with special needs for so long, I understood how people with Asperger's could latch onto people and things.

I did wonder if the problem lay with me. After all, that was what Frank was consistently drilling into to me. So, I turned to my next 'alternative therapy', thinking that it was the menopause up to her nasty tricks again. I contacted a lady in Devon who treated the 'whole' person with herbal remedies that she had grown in her own garden. It was awfully expensive! The lady asked for a full account of my life story up until that point, including all illnesses, all traumas, even wanting to know how often I went to the toilet! I also had to keep a food and drink diary. My stepmother kindly paid for my first consultation and the first load of drugs, which the lady sent to me by post. This came in the form of a tincture and a flower remedy. I took over ordering and paying for it after that.

Every time I tried the next 'therapy', Frank would get all hopeful that I would be 'cured'. First with the oestrogen cream, then with the herb lady and finally with the counselling, which came later. The only problem with that was that he wanted these people to tell me that all his new behaviours, like excessive drinking and hanging around with other women, was okay, and he seemed genuinely perplexed that they did not. If only I had known then what I know now. I was not going to be perfectly 'at peace' until I had rid the world of the dreadful Melissa, where she could not cause any more harm. I really could have saved a lot of time, money, and heartache.

Chapter 11

I do not think I have told you Melissa's surname. It was Trollope! Can you believe my luck? I like to think that it was given to me, and her, as a gift. Ha! I am doubled over laughing at this point. Anyway, back to the story. Once a month, I went out with some other passenger assistants that I used to work with but who have since retired. Chantelle, Carole, and Chris. I am sorry that they are all 'C' names, but what can I do? Well, one evening we went out for a meal and I asked Chantelle if she knew Melissa, as Melissa used to live in the same village, and it turned out that she did! I could not believe it. They had lived around the corner from each other.

I told the girls about the bad feeling I had about Melissa, and Chantelle told me to be careful. Well, Chantelle is not one to gossip or to talk unkindly about people, so I found this a bit worrying. I told them a little bit of how Frank was getting obsessed with Melissa and Nick and that I wondered if Melissa was 'after' my husband. They all emphatically stated that they did not think that Frank was willing or able to hurt me, so I felt slightly reassured. This was the first time that I had expressed my concerns to anybody, but somehow saying it out loud made it even more plausible. I felt like I had a lump of dough in my gut all the time and it just would not budge.

Chantelle also told me that Melissa had no friends (just like Frank). Melissa herself had told me that in our garden – that she had no friends. Chantelle told me that Melissa did used to have two friends in the village, but that they had fallen out. I now wonder if this was because she had made a pass at one or both of their husbands. I am very sceptical of any woman who has no friends. I find this very unusual. All the women I have ever known have liked and needed the company of other women. This is a safe platform, where women talk about their men, their children and sometimes sex. There is an emotional network that I have found with my female friends, which is different to the one I have with my male friends. There is nothing wrong with any of my male friends, I value them all, they just bring something different to the party.

I very stupidly told Frank about what Chantelle had told me at dinner. I also questioned why he thought Melissa had no friends and asked if he found that odd. Unbeknown to me, he was feeding this all back to her, and she would confront me with it later. The betrayals just kept coming. There was nothing I could discuss with him privately anymore. I found it heartbreaking. Prior to all of this, Frank and I were *so* close and were able to discuss anything. So, the next time I saw Melissa, she knocked tentatively on my back door and asked if she could come in. I could tell already that this was a conversation that I would not enjoy having. Meanwhile, Frank and Nick stayed chatting in our garden.

She kicked it all off by saying, "I know that you don't like me."

I said, "It is not that, it is just that Frank talks about you all the time and I am finding it really hard to deal with."

She said, "And he's told me what Chantelle said to you and it made me cry."

I said, "Well Frank should not be discussing with you, what I have talked to him about, and I am sorry if it made you cry." At this point, I did care that it made her cry, but I was currently reeling from Frank's betrayal – again.

And now here comes one of my favourite Melissa quotes (there are more to come…): "Women have hated me all of my life, but I can't help looking like this!"

Well, I was totally flabbergasted! Imagine how hard it must be to be so exceptionally good looking! I can only dream of how difficult this must be.

Anyway, we tried to make some sort of peace treaty, but I just wanted her to leave ASAP. When she left, I ran upstairs and cried my eyes out. Frank came in and asked what had happened and he did not care that he had betrayed my trust, yet again. I told him Melissa's comment about her never having had any friends, and that she could not help looking like that. He did have the good grace, but only on this one occasion, to say that she should not have said it and that it made her sound a bit 'up herself'. No shit, Sherlock.

***

And, so, mine and Frank's relationship went for never having a cross word in 17 years to a constant round of arguing, then me crying and then him trying to twist it to make it seem like I was mental. I spent such a lot of time crying. When I am gut-wrenchingly upset, I end up being sick. I do not know why it happens, but it has happened throughout my life, so you will know when I am really upset because this is what happens. Frank had only seen it happen twice in the previous ten years — once when my daughter said that she wanted to go and live with her father and another time when my cat, Maisie, was poisoned with anti-freeze. Now I was crying regularly and throwing up regularly. As time went on and our relationship became even more volatile, he would later accuse me of 'pretending' to be sick. Another untrue and heart-breaking accusation. But now I am not even sure if this accusation came from him.

As with Daisy, Frank had become secretive with his phone, and he was now even worse. I know that he and Melissa were talking about me behind my back. Of course, I resorted to trying to read his messages when he was not looking. Before this happened to me, I would have been disgusted with the very idea of looking at my partner's phone, but he had made me into such a paranoid mess that I did not even recognise myself anymore. When he found out that I had been looking at his phone, yet more arguments would ensue as he would accuse me of checking up on him and of *me* being deceitful. I have learned since that this is the behaviour of a true narcissist. He would then take to putting his phone on silent so that I would not hear it go off, or changing his pin number so that I could not get into it.

My argument with this is, if you are in a partnership with someone, as though you are a spouse, then you should be able to trust them implicitly and it should perfectly 'safe' for you to be able to leave your phone lying around and for the other party to be able to look at your phone, as you should have nothing to hide and nothing to feel ashamed about them reading. I put this to Frank, who used to leave his phone lying around everywhere, but who now had it practically glued to his person. He used this as a massive gaslighting opportunity to call me 'paranoid', 'suspicious', 'untrustworthy', and 'mental'. And I was beginning to believe every word.

He took to 'working in the shed' increasingly frequently. I would hear him in there talking on his phone. On one occasion, I heard him talking to Rosie, telling her that he was concerned for my mental health and telling her that I was having some sort of mental breakdown. He managed to convince both of my children that the problem lay with me and that he was doing nothing wrong. And they believed him. I cannot blame them, as I believed him too. Of course, it made me stand quietly outside the door of his shed, trying to listen and I can only apologise if you do think that is crazy, but I wanted to hear who else he was talking to, and what other lies he was telling people about me. Trust me, you would have done it too.

Our invites to Melissa and Nick's increased to a level where we were at least seeing them every other weekend. This would cause me extreme anxiety and sleepless nights worrying about it, wondering what I should wear, and when, if ever, I would get a break from Frank talking about them, wanting to see them and us arguing about seeing them. The more this went on, the more Frank drank and drank. We had a bar in our garden and now Melissa and Nick were having a bar and games room built into their house. What was there for Frank not to like? Waiting for their pool table to arrive was like waiting to be executed. I had a strong conviction that I was going to lose him.

We also met up with them a few times in the Conservative club where, after drinks, we would all go upstairs and Melissa, Nick and Frank played pool. I had a misspent youth but, unfortunately, none of it went on me learning to play pool, so I used to have to sit and watch. It did make me feel like a spare doodah at a wedding. One of these times, Melissa asked me how Rosie was as she was breaking up with her then boyfriend. So, obviously, Frank had shared that news with her too then. I said that Rosie was really upset, to which Melissa said, "God, you're *so* maternal!" Like there was something fundamentally wrong with me.

The first time we went upstairs with them I could see how much Melissa revelled in the company of men. She was wearing a woollen tank top that you could see her bra through, and a short leather skirt. So you can just imagine the view when she bent over the pool table. I did tell Frank when we got home that I thought Melissa dressed a little provocatively, but, of course, he said that he had not noticed! This was a recurring theme. He would not or did not want to notice anything that she did. Then, of course, I was accused of being 'nasty' – 'how dare I talk about his friend like that!' He was so very defensive of her all the time, which really did not help. I was not allowed to say *anything* at all about her. He asked how I would feel if he criticised my friends, but I said he could knock himself out if he could name any of my friends that dressed like that, but he could not, because they did not.

By the time their bar was constructed, and they had their full-size proper pool table delivered, mine and Frank's marriage was on the rocks. I really did try with Melissa as I knew how much Frank rated her as a friend, but she made it increasingly difficult. One time we went round and they had a friend of Nick's there – Ivan, and his wife, Terrie. We had already been told that Ivan had known Melissa since school and had 'always fancied her', so she flirted around him outrageously and even sat on his knee at some point. I mean, who would do that? It was cruel to Ivan, and I also felt sorry for Terrie, as it was so disrespectful. I have never before, or since, met a woman like this – who overtly flaunted their sexuality right in people's faces.

Another time, Frank and I were walking to the local shops and we saw Melissa in the back of another taxi driver's newly refurbished camper van. He was called Tony. She was in there wearing shorts that even Kylie Minogue would have thought a bit small and had a vest top on that did not leave much to the imagination. Again, I could see that Tony was loving the attention Melissa was giving him. This time, I decided not to say anything. As it turns out, I did not need to, as apparently Nick had said, "Why does Tony always come around when he knows I am at work?" I did get a bit of pleasure from that when Frank relayed that story back to me.

There are such a lot of incidences to tell you about, I could ramble on for days, but I will try not to bore you unnecessarily. Let me just tell you about the time that we went there and they were watching and listening to a music channel on their big TV in the games room. It would come as no surprise to anybody that knows me that I love Robbie Williams and there is not much I do not know about him, being, as I am, one of his biggest fans. I know a lot of people do not like him as he comes across as arrogant, but I do know that he suffers terribly with social anxiety and I have read that before most of his concerts he can be found throwing up violently in the toilet because he is so nervous.

So, the Robbie that you see performing and 'bigging himself up' is an act to help him conquer his nerves before a performance. Frank and I had been to see him a few times and Frank really enjoyed his concerts and learned to love him as much as I do. He had a Robbie Williams CD in his car and he would sing along to the songs. He knew all the words to a record called 'Me and my Monkey', which is seven minutes long! Even I cannot recite the lyrics of it word for word.

Melissa looked up and said, "I hate him. He is so arrogant." I do not know if she knew how much I like him, so I decided not to bite.

Several months later, I was watching Robbie at home and Frank said, "I hate him. He is so arrogant." You could have knocked me down with a feather. I was so shocked! The more time Frank spent with Melissa, the more that he agreed with everything that she said. It was like he was *becoming* her. I found this very strange and worrying.

My reality was becoming increasingly warped. I did not know fact from fiction. Frank even told me that I should not trust him with his phone because he *was* being secretive! And then when he caught me checking his phone, he would be angry. It was such a confusing time. It was like watching my marriage go down the Swanee, and there was nothing I could do to stop it. I was convinced, after a period of time, that Melissa was making a play for Frank. She kept inviting us to theirs once the games room was complete and their pool table finally arrived. She, Nick, and Frank would play mini tournaments. If Nick lost, Melissa and Frank would make fun of him, and I used to try to defend him because I knew he would not do it himself. One evening, Melissa was deliberately provocative and leant against the wall rubbing one bare foot up and down her other bare leg. Of course, I was the only one that noticed – or was I?

Chapter 12

I was not going to talk about this, but I have decided that you need to know what a bad person I am so you will understand that it is not too difficult for me to recognise the bad in someone else. I had an affair. There, I have said it. I left Tom for Frank, and to make it worse his wife, Sharon, was my friend. There is nothing more wicked or disgusting that a human being can do to another person, and if I were given the opportunity to go back and do things differently, I would take it. Lots of people do not know this about me, and they are going to be shocked. Well, pour yourself a glass and remain seated…

Like I said, I do think that Tom and I both had unresolved traumas from childhood. But this is in no way me trying to justify my level of betrayal. The disgust that I feel for myself is truly palpable. There are some things that are unforgiveable, and this is one of them. I did love Tom and genuinely meant my marriage vows at that time. We had a lot of good come out of our marriage, our beautiful children, James and Rosie, and at my time of writing we have an amazing granddaughter and a grandson on the way. I do hope that, over the passage of time, Tom will find it in his heart to forgive me. He was in no way perfect, neither was I, but I should have tried harder to save our marriage.

I think that if you do not try to keep your marriage alive and make time for each other, then this is sadly the downfall of many a relationship. As my own childhood was so erratic and unstable, as soon as our children came along, I completely forgot about mine and Tom's relationship. I neglected it so that I could be the best mother that I thought it possible to be. I wanted my children to have the best mother ever, even if that meant that I forgot about me or Tom or anything else. I completely lost my sense of self as I tried to forge a way through parenthood.

I was telling my friend, Sharon, about Tom, myself, and the children going on a camping trip to France and she happened to mention that they were also thinking of going to the same place. Sharon suggested that we all go together, whereupon I said that I did not think it was a clever idea as I had a feeling that her husband, Frank, did not like me! But she assured me that it would be fine. Prior to the holiday, I found Frank to be quite 'cold' and miserable (I know, there go those red flags again, that I am *so* going to ignore). So, we all duly went on holiday together. It was a strange set of circumstances. Tom does not enjoy the sun and I have always been a sun-worshipper. So, Frank and I were quite happy to sunbathe while Tom and Sharon sat reading. I am such a child, having never grown up fully after the age of nine, so also enjoy waterparks, as did Frank and the children. So we bonded over our love of the same activities.

Frank and I were both happy to sit up at night chatting and drinking (even then Frank really enjoyed a drink – still no flags!), so we ended up becoming quite good friends. This was a shock to me and, as would later transpire, a shock to everyone else. My previous dealings with Frank had resulted in me crying on at least three occasions. Once he even said something derogatory about my appearance and made me feel uncomfortable. I was soon to discover that Frank was super critical of everybody.

One night, Frank and I oversaw the barbecue whilst Sharon and Tom took the children for a walk and everybody's sausages rolled off onto the grass and became covered in grass and soil. We laughed so much. We decided not to tell the others, so they had gritty sausages on their return, which made us laugh even more. If nothing else, my sense of humour is about the only functioning thing I have that works as it should, and I find humour in a lot of things that most people would not, and the more inappropriate, the funnier I find it…

Nothing at all happened between us on holiday, but we did become fond of each other in the time we were away. So much so that when it was time to leave, I was really upset, and I cried because I did not want it to end. In retrospect, I guess I had been bored with my ordinary life and then this had been 'different' and 'exciting' but really, what was I thinking? I must have taken leave of my senses. I clearly was not thinking straight. When we all got home, I texted Frank and we had only met up three times before I told Tom I was leaving him.

I feel sick to my stomach. I do not blame you if you hate me. I am a bad person and nobody hates me more than I hate myself for what I did to Tom and my children. Not failing to mention what we did to Sharon, and to hers and Frank's children. It was selfish and self-serving, and, as it now appears, achieved absolutely nothing. I have now wasted 18 years of my life that I will never get back. And just to be with Frank, whom I now question as to whether he even loved me at all. But this is my punishment, so I will attempt to take it on the chin. I am not, however, a total pushover and Melissa pushed me beyond the realms of human endurance.

I understand now why our relationship had not worked; it was built on sand. Our foundation had been unsound. It was built on adultery; how can there be mutual trust when we are both clearly untrustworthy? Sometimes I am in a reflective mood, thinking about what I have done that could have caused the following events to occur. I am accepting of some of the blame; I know that I can be a terrible nagger.

I was not the first of Frank's dalliances outside of marriage. Before leaving Sharon, he had also met up with an old school friend and they very nearly had an affair. Frank told me that they would have got together if she had wanted to, but she, rather sensibly, decided not to leave her husband for him. Does Frank have a problem with any sort of long-term commitment? Sadly, we will not find out yet. We could have waited to see if he and Melissa would have lasted – I doubt it, as they are both serial adulterers – only now I have gone and killed her, which is a bit of a bummer.

I told Melissa, once, about mine and Frank's adultery. I brought her into the conversation too and pointed out that she too had committed adultery. She was very defensive, and didn't like hearing it at all. But if you have done something wrong in your life you need to own it otherwise how will you learn and grow and hopefully come out at the other end as a better person? I always expected things to end badly, or to be short-lived with Frank; it was so enthusiastic and intense in the beginning, how could that possibly be maintained? The cancer and the resulting lack of intimacy killed our 'love'. If that is what it even was. Melissa did not help; it was evil what she did. One day, when I am old and frail. I might look back and say, "I fell in love with a man who was my all, my everything, my soulmate, and the other half of me." And not feel this depth of pain, regret, and heartache as I do today.

***

Once, I think Frank may have loved me, but then I got cancer and we could not survive it. Love is not all hearts and flowers and golden Labradors running through fields of wheat, it is not even about good, enthusiastic sex. It is about endurance, it is about moving forward together, defeating all obstacles together, as a team. Love is unconditional. Real love is when you grasp the nettles with both hands, even though it hurts. I tried, in vain, to explain to Frank that love is not a 'feeling'; we have all had that 'feeling' when we fancy someone or when we are in the honeymoon period. This does not last. Love is an action. 'I *will* love you despite your flaws', 'I *will* love you even though I want to kill you sometimes', 'I *will* love you even though you have had cancer surgery'.

At the end of my story, you are within your rights to think that I deserve everything that has subsequently happened to me. That is your prerogative. But, if it helps you to decide, please at least believe that I have felt tremendous guilt for the pain that I caused everybody when Frank and I got together. I do hope that you will see that I did not deliberately cause pain to others and I still feel deep regret. This is much different to how Melissa operated; she was on a mission to destroy mine and my children's lives. She did it with no conscience, or feelings of remorse. She made a concerted effort to destroy everything that I held dear, and I still do not understand why.

When I reflect on it now, Frank was like a lamb led to the slaughter. She made herself irresistible. Through her actions, through her words, through her 'understanding', when his wife – i.e. me – 'didn't understand him' (that 'old chestnut', which has been going on since time immemorial). She did not love him, nor he her; this was a game for her and attention for him. I have learned that a lot of men are weak delicate creatures that mostly operate through their penises. You need to know that I have worked in nursing homes and have been unfortunate enough to look after elderly men at the end of their lives when their testicles have mostly dropped to their knees and their penises have shrivelled up like an over-ripe banana, but they *still* attempt to grope you when you bend over.

Give it a rest, Grandpa, that ship has sailed...

Chapter 13

As I have already explained, my friends are important to me, and I love them all dearly. However, I have a problem with unburdening myself on them as I am aware that everybody has their own problems in life, and I do not like to be a burden. That is probably my own fault and I am not giving them enough credit as I know, in my heart of hearts, that they would be there for me no matter what. But, throughout my life, *I* seem to be the friend that people turn to in a crisis, which always makes me slightly amused, as I do not take my own advice and, so far, my life has been a giant train wreck.

So, for this reason, I did not go to any of my friends with the problems I was having. For a start, Frank made me think that I had gone mad, and I genuinely thought that I was, so I was concerned that my friends might think that I had gone mad too. Everybody thought that Frank and I were a strong couple and that nothing could ever go wrong. I did confide in my friend, Sharon (not Frank's ex), that I was suffering badly with the menopause, and so was she. So, up until I was arrested, we had been phoning each other every Wednesday evening to talk and to vent about our menopausal symptoms. For Sharon, I will be eternally grateful.

I tried to talk to Frank about how the menopause was affecting me and how I was feeling but, of course, he had talked to Melissa about that too and said to me that Melissa had said that she 'sailed through the menopause', so why couldn't I?

In retrospect, I assume it is because she was not even human. Up until all these events, I had believed that Frank loved me and he did do some very loving and kind things for me throughout our marriage, so the subsequent events proved to be very puzzling and alien to me.

For some months, I tried as best as I could to cope with what was going on. I tried to 'be nice' to Melissa. I tried not to 'nag' Frank too much. I tried to pretend that I was happy to go to their house, even though I hated it. Melissa continued to be provocative; I tried not to bite. I tried not to say anything. I pretended to be jolly. It was all extremely arduous work. Melissa would do things to deliberately antagonise me. One day she came to pick Frank up to take him to the garage to collect his car after it had a service. We were both looking out of the lounge window waiting for her to pick him up; it was not that warm but she was wearing her little shorts and a vest top. Frank and I laughed about it. I said, "Tell Melissa she will catch her death, wearing that in this weather."

When he came back, he said that Melissa had said to him, "I bet *she* had something to say about what I was wearing."

I knew at this point that everything Melissa did was her trying to antagonise me, but Frank still could not see it!

Frank and I managed to get through Christmas 2021, but it was not easy. I bought him a lighter on which I had engraved 'I will always love you' because I knew intuitively that our relationship was ending. Even though I prayed hard and begged God for it not to be. God did listen, but He does not always give us everything we want. Like an earthly father, even

He sometimes says no. I was determined that the following year would be different, and I did not want Melissa to destroy us as I still loved Frank and thought that what we had was too precious to lose. So I sent Melissa a message saying that I hope she and Nick had a good Christmas and wished them a Happy New Year.

We arranged to meet up in our local Wetherspoons to clear the air. I was incredibly open with her. I told her about mine and Frank's lack of sexual intimacy and said that it really hurt me. She told me that sex 'dies off' once you have been married for a long time. Well, thank you for trying to educate me (and, yes, it does with 'normal' people, but it should not have with us). I told her how close Frank and I once were. I explained my problems with Daisy and she agreed with me that his relationship with her was inappropriate and said that she had told him so. She said that she was not interested in sex either since she had had breast cancer and that she and Nick did not have any intimacy. She told me that I did not need to worry as she was not interested in Frank and said that they were just friends. She told me how much Frank loved me.

I told her all about his Asperger's and that Frank got obsessed with things. I also may have mentioned that he was not very extravagant with money, yet thought nothing of buying ciders for Daisy, of giving her cigarettes or of buying her McDonald's. I thought, at the end of this, that our chat had gone well and left Wetherspoons reassured. What I did not know was that she relayed our entire conversation back to Frank, so that evening he gave me 'both barrels', saying that I had said he was autistic, was 'tight with money' and had spent the entire conversation running him down. She failed to mention how much I said that I loved him.

It really had not been like that. She had thrown me under the bus – again. I was really upset. I am telling you the truth; I did not run him down. Why would I? I loved him. Oh yes, I wanted to kill her even then. Frank and I had been having this argument in his workshop, and I picked up a piece of four-by-two and threatened to go round to her house to have it out with her! Well, he wrestled that piece of wood from me and barred me from leaving, but soon he would not be there to protect her sorry arse.

It was at this point that I knew that I was dealing with a poisonous and evil person. As much as I tried to draw Frank's attention to what this woman was doing, the more he became her protector. I did not understand it then, and I do not understand it now. Why would he be interested in such a nasty piece of work? I begged and pleaded with him to choose me. He did not understand why he could not have me as his wife and her as his friend. I mean, it was not rocket science. I loved him, heart, body and soul, and she was trying to break us up. I did think then, as I think now, that this was some sort of game or sport for her and one that she was determined to win.

The next thing that happened was that he broke off his relationship with Daisy. He said that Melissa had agreed with me that his relationship with Daisy was inappropriate. So, on Melissa's say-so, he asked Daisy not to come around anymore. Just like that! Poor Daisy! I sobbed my heart out. I did not want him to do that, I had just asked him to back off a little. I had been asking him to do this for ages and nothing happened, but when Melissa suggested it, he told Daisy straight away. Having no filter, he just put a stop to her visits. I was really worried about the harm he might have done her, but of course he said, "Now you've got what you wanted, so I do not know why you are upset!"

As our relationship neared its end, Frank would later throw this in my face and said to me in a childish voice, "Daisy was my friend, and you ruined it!" He was almost having a temper tantrum like a two-year-old. Frank, I did not ask you to do that, buttercup – it was Melissa, remember? I will never forget Daisy and I did love her. I used to introduce her to my friends as my adoptive daughter. I hope that she will get to know, one day, that I did not ever ask Frank to stop her coming around anymore and that I will always be here for her, if she needs me.

Things deteriorated again after that. I realised that I could no longer trust either of them. By now, I was convinced that Frank and Melissa were having an affair. And I did accuse him of it daily. He would try to reassure me that he loved me and that, of course, he was not. My gut felt that something was not right. If I could give you any piece of advice it would be to always listen to your gut. After one difficult evening he did tell me that, after I was diagnosed with breast cancer, something in him had 'died'. I was heartbroken. I did suggest that it was not my fault that I had had cancer, in the hope that it would soften his heart towards me, and he did say, "How do you think I feel, as a man, not being able to satisfy my own wife?" And I did feel some compassion towards him, but I will never know if it was then, or later, that he started to have sex with Melissa.

I decided to meet up with Melissa again. If nothing else, God loves a trier! I arranged to meet her in Wetherspoons again, only this time I asked Frank to come with me. I asked him not to tell her but, of course, he did. I could tell by the way that she was not at all shocked to see him sitting with me when she arrived. They both vehemently denied that they were having an affair and assured me they were just friends. They both ganged up on me. She told me she knew that I thought she dressed provocatively; I told her that she did. This is one of the many things that I had discussed with Frank in the privacy of our own home. It was now that I realised that they told each other *everything*. I had never been more hurt in my life.

I was already feeling extremely vulnerable; it was like I had turned up naked and that everybody could see me. Melissa could 'see me' and revelled in my vulnerability. I was like a fly in her web and there was nothing I could do to escape from it. I started to cry. My weakness was exposed for her to see and to enjoy. Frank went to get the cups of tea. When he left, she put her hand gently over mine, looked at me straight in my eyes and said, "Look, I know that I am slender and attractive, but maybe you have other qualities." Well, a large metaphoric hole opened beneath me. I just looked at her. I am not usually lost for words, but there were no words. Frank came back and she quickly removed her hand off my clenched hands on the table and she continued to talk as if were just having as nice friendly chat.

When Frank and I left Wetherspoons, I told him that I had never been so betrayed in my life and that our marriage was over. I could not believe how much he had divulged to her about things that I had confided to him about in the safety of our own home. It was now that, for the first time, I thought about taking my own life. I am sorry if this is upsetting to read, but I had never been so broken. That night, I took the photograph from the wall of all our family – us, and our four children. I got a hammer and told him to smash it up and to put it in the bin, as this is what he was doing to our family. I also took my wedding and engagement rings off, threw them at him and told him to give them to Melissa.

Until the present day, I do not think that he has ever believed that Melissa said those things to me in Wetherspoons. That hurts so much. I had never lied to him and was not about to start. I even got in touch with a lie detector agency to enquire about the price of having a lie detector test, but I should not have had to do that (it would have cost £400, by the way). But she and I know the truth, so if he chooses to believe her over me, he probably would not even believe the test. He so wanted to believe in her. I was not going to get a look-in. Whatever I did, I was not going to win. She had set her stall out and she was better at this than I was. This was not going to end, I decided, until one of us was dead.

***

At some point during the beginning of 2022, I had arranged to go out with Elaine and Ann for a belated Christmas meal. Elaine came to our house to get ready, and I disclosed some of what was going on with Frank and me. She offered to phone him a few days after and I let her, as I really did not understand myself what was going on. I still have the message that she sent me after her discussion with him. Frank had managed to convince her that there was nothing at all going on with him and Melissa.

Frank told her that he was pleased to have Melissa and Nick as friends and that he enjoyed playing pool with them. He told her that his school run took up three hours of every day and that the only way to make it bearable was to have a laugh and a chat with whoever was escorting the child and that just happened to be Melissa. He assured her that he loved me and was just worn out with the distrust and the arguing. She suggested that we go for counselling, and he said that he would. For my benefit, please try to remember everything that I have just told you.

Some weeks later, one of my friends told me that they had seen Frank and Melissa in our car parked in McDonald's car park having a coffee together. This was not during work time. He had the gall to wonder why I was upset! Of course, I rang him and, of course, I went berserk. He made up some lame excuse about her needing a mask (this was during Covid), so he met up with her to give her one – a mask that is. He could not or did not want to see why I was angry and why it was inappropriate. I am no saint and have a temper, but it is a fairly slow burn, but I can use enough profanities to make a nun blush. I am not proud of it. But, yet again, he made out that this was all my fault. What was wrong with me? Why was I so suspicious? They were just friends for goodness sake!

Not for the first time, I asked Frank to give up the school run. He used the excuse that it paid really well, but if he had wanted to save our marriage he would have done. There are more important things than money and I thought our marriage was one of them. Unfortunately, he did not. But was he already having sex with Melissa by now? Melissa, too, knew that our marriage was on very dicey ground and if she had anything decent about her at all, she would have backed off and stopped what she was doing with Frank so that we could save our marriage. It did not take me too long to realise that she had a heart made of stone.

Frank used to get really annoyed if I questioned where Melissa's 'girl code' was. He did not understand that most decent women would have tried to help. Especially as she was forever proclaiming that she was his friend. But the worse things got between Frank and I, the more she invited him around. And as he was flattered or smitten, or whatever, he used to trot round there like a little lamb to the slaughter. It did not matter if I cried or pleaded, he would walk out of the back door without a second thought or a glance back at me to see if I was okay. By now, he would say that I was using 'emotional blackmail' to prevent him from going. Well, after the first time, when he did not care, only a fool would keep on doing that. I was genuinely devastated that he would rather be with Melissa than with me, his wife.

The Frank that I loved and adored for almost 18 years was going. It was like he had died and I was left with a robot replacement. The only thing that they had in common was that they looked the same. The 'robot' Frank was cold, unfeeling, unemotional, hard, stiff, and dismissive. He had said to me the previous summer that throughout his life he had put his emotions inside a suitcase tied up with string, and that he was not ever going to release it because he would not be able to deal with it. He was crying when he said this, and partly blamed his upbringing on not being able to fully express himself. Well, welcome to my world.

He had also said that summer that our marriage would end if I did not let him have his relationship with Daisy and Melissa. Now who had used 'emotional blackmail'? At that time I had said that I would 'try to be better', 'try to be quiet and good'. I guess men do not like it and call women 'crazy' if they do not like them having relationships with other women. To block any emotions thereafter, Frank continued to drink to excess and got addicted to a game on his phone called *Wooduko*, which he played day and night. That is, when he was not writing secretive messages on his phone.

During lockdown and beyond, Frank and I had started going on walks to improve our overall health. We started to argue every time we went for a walk, so eventually we started to go on separate walks. I asked to go with him, but he usually would not let me. I wonder now if he was meeting up with Melissa, as I knew that was how her affair with Nick had started. She used to 'walk her dogs' and meet up with him. Certainly, whenever any of my friends saw Frank out walking, he was always on his phone.

When I went walking, I was usually sobbing at the same time. I used to say to him, "I am just going 'crying-walking'." He did not even look up. I used to stand by the train track, thinking how much easier it would be to just step in front of a moving train, as the pain was so unbearable. Looking back, I was having some sort of mental breakdown. My thoughts about the situation were all tangled up with my grief for my mum and I sometimes did not know which thing I was crying about. I am very secretive and am the world's best actor, so none of my friends knew how bad I was feeling. By now, I had told my stepmum, Trisha, what was going on and she just had to listen while I cried a river day after day. There was nothing she could do except pray that I was going to be all right.

I googled how many paracetamol one needed to take to die successfully and decided to buy four packets of 16 and to hide them in case I needed them. I am ashamed of this now and cannot believe that I even got to this way of thinking when I have children. What would it have done to them? I will never, as long as I live, allow another man to get me in such a place of sorrow and that is a solemn promise. My Frank had been warm, considerate, affectionate, and loving. I did not know who Frank was anymore, or where he had gone. The loss was massive.

Behind the scenes – and I was not to find this out until after subsequent events – Frank was having conversations with my children about how mental I was and that I needed help. Obviously, they were both worried sick. Understandably, they took Frank's side as he had managed to convince them both that there was nothing going on with Melissa and there had not been anything going on with Daisy either. So, like him, they probably thought that I had finally lost all sense of reality. It was easy for them to think. Prior to all this happening, the menopause had made me very emotional and caused my behaviour to be erratic.

Chapter 14

I tried hard to save our marriage. I even went to the Conservative club and watched football with Frank on several occasions. He is a Liverpool supporter and had only just got back into watching them. Even that was a change in his personality. He had not bothered watching any football for years. Of course, the Conservative club also helped him to enjoy a steady flow of alcohol. Is that why he was going? It was all completely different and out of character. I told him that I felt like a ship on the ocean with no clear direction and that I did not feel safe. He did not care.

The night before my birthday, which is on 1st March, Frank, Rosie, and I went out for a meal in Wetherspoons. Even telling you this is putting me right back there, to the very moment when my life was shattered. I do not remember what we had been talking about but, at some point, I put my hand on Frank's leg and said, "You know you love me really."

He replied, "I am not sure I do, actually."

This was when my life totally imploded, right at that moment. I ran out of Wetherspoons, and I was hysterical. Poor Rosie. I was so ashamed of her seeing me like that. We got home and I just cried and cried. When Rosie left, I asked him if it was the end of our marriage and he said that it was, and that it was all over. Not missing the chance, of course, to say that it was my fault because of my jealousy and the fact that he had warned me the year before that this would happen.

That evening, I walked around to my friend Donna's house. I have known Donna since our boys were three and our daughters were babies. She was there with her husband, Dave. They were very shocked to see me and, by now, I must have looked a real mess. Bearing in mind I had not shared any of what had been going on with Frank and I until now, I told them all about Daisy and Melissa and that Frank had ended our marriage. They were very shocked and upset. But, as I expected, they could not have been more supportive. I felt awful for not having opened up to them before then.

It was comforting when I begin to realise that I had not gone mad. They could not believe the extent of the Daisy situation and explained that no woman would have liked it. Dave also could not get his head around why a grown man in his 50s would even want such a close relationship with a young girl and found it distasteful. I was gradually starting to realise that not everything was my fault! Also, they said that Frank's relationship with Melissa was hurting me, so he should have stopped it. This was such a direct contrast to what Frank had been drilling into me for the past few months. I felt so confused. And they said that Melissa should have backed off too! It was like the scales from my eyes were dropping, and I was learning to see.

Donna and Dave promised to help me through this, and they could not have been more encouraging and are still caring for me now. I do not know what they will think of my arrest, but Dave is feisty, too, so I expect he will understand. Though he, out of everybody, has tried to get me to be calm and not to retaliate, so I am sorry for letting him down. When I got home after seeing them, Frank declared that we would now be sleeping in separate bedrooms as our marriage was over. So,

I moved into one of the spare bedrooms and cried all night, while he slept and snored. I should have realised right then, that if a man can sleep when he has broken your heart and turned your life upside down, then he does not love you, at all (it is also likely that he is having sex with somebody else as well, so it turns out).

The next day was my birthday. Frank had not bought me a present and he gave me a generic female birthday card, with no 'wife' on the front, or words of endearment. It would have been kinder not to have bothered. Donna and Dave took me out for lunch, but I spent much of the day crying. Frank's mum, Belinda, phoned me to wish me a happy birthday, as she usually would, and I told her that Frank had ended our marriage. I was hysterical. She was really kind to me, said that she was cross with him, that he had responsibilities, and that he could not do this. I really thought that I had her support. Unfortunately, as it now appears, I thought wrong.

That evening, I got in touch with Jacquie, who is not only my friend, but also my cousin. We have known each other for years, but did not realise we were related until I did my family tree on *Ancestry* and we matched! What are the chances, eh? And I met up with my friend, Linda, too. We three call ourselves 'the Golden Girls' as we are all blonde. They took me to the pub, and they were *so* lovely. Linda cuddled me and I remember Jacquie kissing me on the head. Jacquie was in her pyjamas with just a coat over the top. They dropped everything just to be with me. It is making me feel emotional just remembering it. I told them about it all, but they, and other people, were still doubting that Frank would be cheating on me with Melissa. Part of me still did not believe it. He would have been pleased that so many people had that much faith in him.

But, that night – bearing in mind that it was my birthday and he had ruined my life – he still went to Melissa and Nick's to play pool. I properly lost it when I was home alone. I was uncontrollably distraught and recall sliding down the fridge freezer onto the kitchen floor and I just lay there wanting to die. I, again, begged and pleaded with God to make the pain stop. Even if it meant that he would take my life. I imagined myself ending things and I did not think about what it would do to anybody else, I just did not want to be here.

Poor Trisha, my poor children. All my friends and family, having to listen to me crying day after day. It must have been so awful for them. By now, Rosie was very worried about my mental health and contacted a counsellor, called Rebecca, to see if she would help me. In the meantime, I could not function properly as I felt so broken. Frank called the doctor and told him that I was depressed and suicidal and asked him to sign me off work. The doctor put me on antidepressants and gave me a sick note. Even when Frank was explaining all this to the doctor, he was very cold and said, "She's upset, because I've ended our marriage."

And as upset as I was, Frank was very clinical with the arrangements. He kept pressing me to change the bank account, to separate our mobile telephone bills and kept wanting to talk, saying, "What are we going to do?" I did not care. I loved him and wanted to make it work. I phoned my line manager at work and told her what was going on and told her that the doctor had signed me off sick. She was incredibly supportive. I could not have worked through this, as I was spending 90 per cent of my time crying. I am never again going to let a man reduce me to this.

The next time I talked to Belinda, Frank's mother, she was quite different from the first time I had spoken to her on my birthday. Frank had 'got at her' by now and had managed to turn everything around and blamed me for our marriage going wrong due to my jealousy. She said that he 'only wanted to play pool'. I mean, when you put it like that, playing pool *does* seem pretty innocuous, but there was so much more to it than that. She did not want to see anything from my point of view and had decided that Frank could do no wrong. I get those mothers that take their kids side – I know as I am a mother too. But mine are not perfect, and I would hope that I would err on the side of what is 'right', even if that meant me telling my child that what they have done is wrong.

In fact, she really upset me. I was genuinely terrified as to what was going to become of me. I only had a part-time job with a small income and, of course, I was scared. She said, "Pull yourself together, you will just have to get a full-time job!" If she had any inkling of how much I loved her son, she would have realised that I was having a breakdown. She also told me off for shouting at him and swearing. What did she want me to do? Lay down and die whilst Melissa was making passes at my husband, and he was falling for it? She did say that Frank was willing to go to marriage guidance, but only for one session. Well, that about summed up his commitment to 'us' then, didn't it?

I arranged to go and stay with James and Sofia, but I was not at all well mentally. I could not sleep very well and kept crying all the time. Every morning I went into my son's bedroom in tears. I always woke up crying in the mornings. However, James and Sofia could not have been more kind. I felt so loved and looked after. It was like having a break at a health farm. They fed me well, made sure I was comfortable, and we had lots of walks in the countryside with their dog. Sofia's parents, Jack and Susan, were also really kind to me and took me to and from the train station. Susan said that she felt that Frank was having an affair with Melissa too, and believed that, eventually, my suspicions would prove to be correct.

While I stayed there, I took James and Sofia to York Minster, and I prayed in just about every place therein and on my knees. I prayed that Frank would not leave me and that he was not cheating on me with Melissa. I lit a candle for our love and prayed that it would be enough. I kept sending him photographs of us: wedding photos, happy days out, soppy love poems and recordings of songs that we liked while I was away. I was a shadow of my former self. I did not even care that I was almost begging for him to love me. I was pathetic. Writing this now, I am so furious with myself. No man should have this much emotional power over a woman. But I gave it to him in spades.

Unbeknown to me at that time, Frank had been having conversations with James, telling him to knock some sense into me and to make sure that I understood that it is was all over. How cruel to try to use my son in this way. It is repulsive and disgusting. Out of everything that has happened since, I will never recover from the way he and Melissa hurt my children. Both of my children really loved him and have been devastated by everything that has happened too. This has not just hurt me. Some things are just unforgivable, and this is one of those things.

I still do not understand how Frank was so willing to cast our family aside. He had already hurt his ex-wife, Tilly, and Bradley. Indeed, we both had with our actions – not forgetting Tom and my children too. I am so grateful that God spared me from getting pregnant with our own child, because doubtless he would have walked out on that one too. We did not use any contraception for the first three months of our relationship, because we would have liked to have had a child between us. Thank God nothing happened, as I would now be solely responsible for a teenager with a raft of problems.

When I suggested to Frank that what we had done had harmed our own children, he would get really annoyed with me, but all four of them have had 'issues', one way or another. How could they not? In the natural order of things, children thrive better when their parents remain together. Unless it is a very toxic environment, of course, with massive arguments or violence, but we had neither of these things. I really could not comprehend how it was so awful for him – living with me and maintaining a relationship with my children – and why he thought that it would be better to live alone in a flat. I worried about him feeling lonely, not realising then, that this was not his intention at all.

I have a close male friend called Leigh. He has been like an angel helping me through all that has gone on in the last 18 months. We have known each other since before I married Tom. He said something remarkably interesting to me, and it was refreshing to get a male perspective on the situation. He said, "Men very rarely leave a marriage to be by themselves, there is always somebody else to go to. Men are big babies and cannot survive by themselves. A woman will leave a man and be on her own, but a man will not." Still, even after all that, a big percentage of me did not think that Frank was being unfaithful. I know what you are thinking – what an idiot!

***

Before I had left to go to James and Sofia's, I wrote a love letter to Frank and left it under his pillow to find when he went to bed. In it I declared how much I loved him and the family we had created, how much I did not want our marriage to end, and probably loads more sickly protestations of love that, if I read it now, would cause me to be sick into my own mouth. I will now never know if this is when he first brought Melissa into our bed. He was certainly very keen for me to 'go away' all the time. The day before I was due to come home, he sent me a WhatsApp message saying, *I've missed you this weekend'.* Well, you could have knocked me down with a feather! I was so confused. What did he mean?

I was very astonished to see him smiling at me at the station when I arrived home. He threw his arms around me, said that he had missed me, and I walked back to the car in total amazement. In the car, I said, "What is happening?"

He said, "You do not know what you have got until it is gone!"

As you can imagine, I was internally jumping for joy. I asked him if that meant we were going to make another 'go of it' and he said, "Yes." And we drove home holding hands. I was *so* happy; I could hardly believe it.

When we got home, he asked me what I would like for my birthday as he had not bought me a birthday present and he said that he would buy me an eternity ring and that I could choose it myself. As you will learn, his 'eternity' and my 'eternity' have very different stages of length! I, nor anybody else, would ever get to comprehend these events, as they just do not make any sense. I wonder now if he and Melissa had cooled their relationship and that I was better than nothing? Remember what Leigh had said? Or, had Melissa changed her mind and decided to make a go of things with Nick? There are so many unknowns, it really is frustrating.

However, I was pleased at the time. Common sense and love had won out. We could get our relationship back on track and everything could go back to some sort of normality. I had to contact everybody that I knew about this new change of events and, of course, they were pleased for me. James and Rosie were overjoyed, too, as they loved Frank and wanted us to be back together. What I had not realised was that Frank thought that, as he was kind enough to get back with me, that I would now 'allow him' to do his own thing and to start going to Melissa's increasingly without me saying anything or complaining.

I tried going with him to Melissa and Nick's, but it gradually became more and more difficult. I thought that now we had got back together that his visits there would become less frequent but, if anything, they became much worse. I cannot remember why now, but at some moment in time, I stopped going with him, and Melissa had said that I was no longer welcome. It was very painful to live every day knowing that my husband would rather spend time with other people than with me, his wife. We had increased arguments about it. I told him that he made me feel lower than an earthworm and I still could not see for the life of me what Frank could see in Melissa. I used to say that he must think she was magnificent and that I was not worthy. That is certainly how he made me feel.

I even offered to stop going out with my friends so that we could spend more time together, but he refused, saying I was using 'emotional blackmail'. I really was not. I would have done anything to save our marriage. I continued to go on a lot of 'crying' walks – sometimes in the middle of the night, which he would, again, sleep and snore through, and not even give a thought to. I walked through a dark lane once at midnight, thinking if I got murdered then at least I would be free.

The worst thing about having a husband who lives in the same house as you, but who is emotionally distancing himself from you, is trying to find a moment in the day when you do not relive all the good times you had. It is like an internal video player that just goes on and on. We were back sleeping in the same bed, but there was still no intimacy. The most touching I was permitted was for him to hold on to my hair so that I could sleep. I just needed some human touch, however slight. Can you imagine being this pathetic? We quite often argued into the night and then I would end up crying and throwing up and Frank would end up going downstairs and start drinking. This could go on until the early hours and then a few hours later he would be out driving his taxi. I was worried sick.

I hardly had any sleep. I do not know how I was managing to get through each day. At about this time I heard back from the counsellor, Rebecca, that Rosie had found for me. Rosie chose her based on the photo of her kind face on her portfolio. It was a wonderful choice! Frank was excited that I was going to see a counsellor, as he thought that she would make me see sense and let him do what he liked. He honestly thought that our marital problems were all my fault and did not think that he was doing anything wrong.

I used to talk to myself, saying, "I know that he cannot really be doing this to me. He cannot mean it. Is it because he is an alcoholic and does not know what he is doing anymore? We loved – no, love – each other so much. Will there be no future for us at all?" I could not begin to imagine a life without

Frank in it and I genuinely loved his children and his parents, not to mention the rest of his extended family. I worried excessively about the cats. We both loved them. If we split, where would they go? Who would they go with? Would we be allowed them if we rented somewhere?

Chapter 15

Every time I went 'crying-walking' I would bump into Melissa. She would be out walking her dogs and was always on her mobile phone. I would think of a reason to phone Frank once I passed her, to see if his phone was also engaged and, often, it was. Every time I saw her, I felt sick. I would go hot and sweaty and could feel bile rise into the back of my throat. One morning, as I was walking to my first appointment to meet Rebecca, I saw her walking some way ahead of me.

Even though she had her back towards me, I could recognise her straggly deep brown, almost-black hair anywhere. She had lost weight. *Bikini-ready for the summer*, said Frank in my head. This was something she had said to him previously. "I am going on a diet, so that I can be bikini-ready for the summer." Why did Frank find it necessary to tell me these things? She was wearing a little vest top again, and small denim shorts. She was walking like a catwalk model, with a confident stride, like she was ready to conquer the world.

She was tilting her head from side to side, with her long hair moving rhythmically over her shoulders. She turned and saw me; it must have been by sixth sense. How did she know that I was there? I quickly dodged to the right, even though I did not need to go that way, and ended-up in a 'no-through' road. I had to jump off a wall once I reached a dead end. I could not believe myself the anxiety that she was able to provoke in me. I could feel panic rising. Why did she have this effect on me? My palms went clammy, and I was even shaking. I did not know if it was caused by anger or hatred, or both, but certainly she triggered fear in me.

So, by the time I arrived at Rebecca's house for my first counselling session, I was very on edge. When Rebecca first opened her front door to me and she smiled, I could feel genuine kindness and warmth. She had warm brown eyes and soft features. I knew immediately that I could trust her, which is just as well, as I spent most of the first session sobbing and rocking and covered in snot. She just put a box of tissues in front of me and let me cry. It was a huge release. I did not know that I had that many tears left. She said that she felt that she could help me if I would let her. There was something about her that gave me absolute trust in the process, so, of course, I said that I would see her again.

That evening, Frank asked me how I got on. I could feel that he wanted Rebecca to have told me that I was being unreasonable but at this point she and I had not been able to talk about my problems because, as I have said, I spent most of that first session as a blubbering mess. So, my life continued in a very dysfunctional manner. Frank kept going out and I kept crying and being sick. We would argue and I would beg him to 'choose' me. I could be hysterical and he would just shout, "Bye!" as he left, without turning back. Melissa had made me feel so small and insignificant, like I was an earthworm trying to rise through the earth, and then she would wait and, with a sly smile, metaphorically stamp on me.

I had a very unpleasant experience one day when I was walking back to my house with my friend, Lin. We had met up for coffee at our local shopping centre. As we started to proceed along the road, Melissa was walking on the other side of the road. I quietly said to Lin, "That's Melissa." (Lin knew all about what had gone on).

Well, Melissa must have extremely good hearing because, when she got to the end of the road, she shouted, "I EXPECT YOU'RE TELLING HER THAT I'M HAVING AN AFFAIR WITH YOUR HUSBAND?" This was loud, like an old fishwife, and extremely embarrassing. Apart from anything else, I felt really shaken by it. Lin had to come in my house with me and try to calm me down.

Lin said that she had never witnessed anything like it, and concluded that Melissa must be crazy. Us both not realising then that Melissa was at least wanting to sleep with my husband, if she had not already, which makes her shouting that out even more bizarre. 'Methinks the lady doth protest too much'. Lin left and I phoned Frank and told him what had happened, and he did not make much of it at all, or care that I was shaken. I began to realise that anything Melissa did was all fine by him and that anything I did was annoying or ridiculous. Where had our 18 years of loving each other gone? Had Frank ever really loved me? Did I not know the real Frank? Was this the real Frank?

***

Between then and May of last year, we were preparing to go to James and Sofia's wedding. I bought myself a new outfit and Frank had a new tie, cufflinks, and a tie pin. I had his suit dry cleaned. It should have been an exciting time, but it was marred by Frank's continual going out to spend time at Melissa and Nick's. I could tell that Frank was not invested in my son's wedding and I found it hurtful. He continued to drink excessively, and he had even started to hide evidence of his drinking. He spent a lot of time in his workshop and there was not a lot of activity coming from there. I found a bottle of vodka hidden in a cupboard in there, and a crate of Pepsi covered with a blanket.

I was, by now, keeping my friends and family in the loop as to what was going on. I had told them that Frank's personality had completely altered, and I just did not know who he was anymore. There were many different theories. Several people suggested that he had a brain tumour and that he could not help it. Other's thought that he had a terminal illness and did not want to tell anybody. Was he just an alcoholic and the drink had changed his thinking? Was he simply having a mid-life crisis? I used to say to him repeatedly, "Where have you gone?" or "Who are you?" I guess we will never get to find out what caused all of this, unless I hear that he has died or something, and someone tells me that he did, in fact, have a brain tumour. I even asked him if he was gay and if he was struggling with his sexuality, I told him that if he were, we would be able to work through it together.

When I split up with Tom, he had said that he would much prefer it if I had died. For the first time, I fully got what he meant. If Frank had died, of course, I would have been heartbroken, but it would not have been his fault; but with this, he was *choosing* to treat me like this. We did not talk to each other, unless we were arguing, and the rest of the time he sat playing *Wooduko* on his phone. There are not enough adjectives to fully describe how lonely and unloved I felt. I decided that Frank's behaviour toward me was far crueller that Tom had ever been and that really shook me to the core.

Frank completely rejected me in the bedroom now. He refused to cuddle me, but would still hold my hair if I pleaded with him. Oh, the shame! I used to say to him that I felt like a Victorian pauper, begging for some crumbs from his table and that is exactly what it was like. I had previously worshipped Frank from an extremely high pedestal, which he knew, and which he now exploited at every turn. In a moment of kindness, he did say to me that I was the best wife any man could ever wish for and had been the best stepmother to his kids that he could have ever asked for. And he wondered why people might have thought that he had a brain tumour! It was such a confusing time. He also agreed with me that nobody could love him like I did, so why would you opt to throw that all away? I am still waiting for someone to love me like that.

If I love somebody, it does not come with conditions. I love you and am willing to look past your flaws. Of course, Frank was not a perfect human being, and neither am I, but I loved him despite his funny ways and, sometimes, because of them. But it seemed now that Frank only loved me if I was willing to share him with other women and he wanted me to smile and be happy about it whilst he did so. Previously, I did believe that he loved me unconditionally, so this was another thing that I had to try to come to terms with because, as it appears, he did not.

The night before James and Sofia's wedding, my stepmother, Trisha, stayed at our house, as we were travelling up to North Yorkshire together. Things were still the same with Frank and I, and the atmosphere at home was terrible. As per the rest of our marriage, I tried to excuse his behaviour, which was sullen and moody, by saying that he must be thinking about the long drive. I also told her that Frank was not looking forward to seeing Tom, who would also be there with his new family, so obviously it was quite an awkward situation.

Frank spent that evening on his phone, I assume playing *Wooduko*, but was he in fact talking to Melissa? Because he did not interact with us at all. The journey up there was uncomfortable and quiet, so I talked nonsense, which is what I do to fill in any embarrassing gaps in the conversation. When Frank left the car to pay for fuel, Trisha asked me what was going on with him. I wish I had known. I will never understand why Frank came to the wedding when he so clearly did not want to be there. Later he informed me that he did it for James', which would have been nice if he had tried to participate in anything. Poor James, he too had really felt Frank's love before, but it was fast disappearing.

Obviously, being the groom's mother, I was distracted by the emotions of the day and did not fully appreciate what was going on as I was more interested in seeing James and Sofia have a lovely wedding day. Since the wedding, though, everybody has told me how miserable Frank was, how he did not interact with anybody and was displaying an act of disinterest with everything. I am now 100 per cent convinced that Frank and Melissa's sexual relationship was happening at this time.

In our hotel room, he was cold and unfeeling towards me. He would not cuddle me or even put his arm around me. I started to cry, and he played with his phone. The person who I had thought loved me the most was now being the cruellest person I had ever met. I asked him to have some empathy for me as a fellow human being, if not as his wife, but he was not even capable of that. After the wedding, I have been told that Sofia's father said to her mother, "I would put money on the fact that Frank will end their marriage when they get home."

James and Sofia's wedding was wonderful. James' godmother and my good friend, Fiona, and her husband had travelled all the way from Watford to attend and it was lovely to see them. My brother, Christian, was also there with his girlfriend, Laura, and they had flown all the way from Spain to come to the wedding. So, some parts of it were joyous for me. Also, Rosie was bridesmaid and she looked beautiful. James and Sofia really love each other so it was a moving and holy day in a stunning church filled with a lot of people celebrating a glorious occasion. Frank spent the entire day with a face like a bag of spanners. But was he missing Melissa and was she not liking him coming away for the weekend with his wife? Again, we will never really know.

During the vows, I held Frank's hand and felt emotional. I was hoping that he would feel the same as, each time a vow was said, I squeezed his hand. I really needed some reassurance from him that we were going to be okay after that blip that we had had in March. Sofia made a stunning bride and James looked so smart in his suit. I honestly could not have felt prouder of them both. At the reception, Frank produced a bottle of vodka from the inside pocket of his suit, which he proceeded to drink and, again, did not socialise with anybody. And most of the evening I did not even know where he was. My brother invited us over to Spain, which Frank, who normally loves a holiday, would usually enthuse about, but now would not commit to.

Chapter 16

We had only been home from James and Sofia's wedding for two days when Frank ended our marriage for good. He said that he was not going to change his mind this time. I asked him what the U-turn had been about in March, about how he was when he picked me up from the station, and the fact that he had bought me an eternity ring. He said that he had really tried to make things work and said that he thought if he put a handbrake on our relationship, then *I* might change! I told him that I also thought that *he* would change and would stop putting Melissa ahead of me. Since March, nothing had altered except that he would now go to Nick and Melissa's even more then he had been.

He used to get so angry when I said that he thought more of Melissa than he did of me. But what did he expect me to think? Melissa stepped up the invites to their house and he now went there every Saturday without fail, leaving me at home crying, without a hint of remorse. He was so *desperate* to go there that he used to leave at ten to seven precisely, so that he would be there at exactly seven, which was the time that Melissa summoned him to go there. I used to watch him get ready. He was much more appearance-focussed now. One evening, he spent a whole ten minutes doing his hair! It cut like a knife when I watched him splash on the aftershave that *I* had bought him for Christmas before going out.

Sometimes I used to go out before he left so that I would not have to see him leave to go to *her* house as I found it too upsetting. Other times I would just wait for him to leave and spend the rest of the evening crying and drinking gin (this is not to be recommended as I do think it makes you feel worse). Frank would claim that he was just going there to 'play pool', but I still had this extraordinarily strong gut feeling that he was really going there to see Melissa. I was still asking him if they were having an affair but it was always met with extremely angry and strong denials and him telling me that I was mentally ill and needed to get some help. Now I have learned about gaslighting, this all makes sense.

I still felt suicidal. Our children all had their own lives. My life now felt worthless and I did not feel as if there was any purpose to it. I had spent so long loving Frank that I did not know anything else. My own needs did not figure in my life at all. I was still very afraid of being by myself and could not imagine that I would be able to cope living on my own. I did feel that Frank was being cruel and selfish, knowing my history as he did. My future just looked so bleak. I really did not know what I was going to do. I asked Frank what I was supposed to do if my cancer came back – that is a massive fear of anybody who has had a scare or who has had cancer and is remission – but I was just accused of emotional blackmail.

As the weeks went by, I was becoming increasingly ill with the stress and worry of it all. I hardly slept, thinking about what I was going to do and how I would get through this. I could not come to terms with Melissa's cruelty either. She was a woman – she should have been on my side. She knew the difficulties we were having and instead of trying to help our marriage, she was sabotaging it with these constant invites. One day, while I was out crying-walking, I passed her again and I know I must have looked awful. Frank told me that night that Melissa had seen me and she had said that she felt sorry for me because I was about to lose everything!

As if I had not realised it before, I now fully appreciated that I was not dealing with a normal human being. Like Frank, she had no empathy. Maybe this is one of the reasons that they were attracted to each other? Melissa is not at all maternal and Frank is not overly paternal. They do not get involved in anything that requires any genuine emotion. In me, Frank had married the most emotional person in the world. Was he bored of my feelings? I admit that I am a bit much for people to deal with – God knows I find myself difficult, but he knew what I was like when we got together. He once told me that I was the kindest person he had ever met. Go figure. He also once told Trisha that I did not have a nasty bone in my body. Well, he got that wrong.

I was now seeing Rebecca every week. This sounds a bit dramatic, but I think she may have saved my life. She could fully appreciate everything I was saying, she did not blame me for how I was feeling, she said that I was 'normal'. Hurray! She said that no woman would have liked the relationship that Frank had with Daisy or Melissa. She said that if Melissa had been any sort of decent human being, she would have said to Frank, "To help you save your marriage, I will back off and not invite you around anymore." But, no, Melissa invited him around even more.

Rebecca always gave me 'homework'. I am not good at it, unless I have a deadline. That's ADHD again. But sometimes I really did do it and a couple of times I showed it to Frank, who was not interested now as, in his view, Rebecca should have told me that his behaviour was acceptable. It was so nice having somebody neutral that could help me make sense of it all. We did go right back to my childhood experiences that had led me to the place where I now had two failed marriages and she concluded that as my parents were not 'safe' people. I had subconsciously chosen partners who could not meet my emotional needs as that is what I was used to and that is what I had thought love was. Rebecca said that now I knew all this, I could make better choices in the future. Well, we will see, but I need to get my 'red flag' sensor up and running first, as it has been seriously defunct.

I also realised that I had 'got stuck' at the age of nine and had not grown up. I found this really interesting, as I have always said that inside I feel like I am nine, even before I met Rebecca! This was the age I was when my grandparents moved away and when I lived with my dad by ourselves and he used to leave me on my own a lot. This also explained why, as a grown woman of 50-plus, I feared being in the house by myself and feared the dark. This is embarrassing even sharing this, but it might help somebody else if they feel the same.

I had to do a lot of work on myself. I had to write letters to my 'inner child', telling her that I would get through this, to be brave and that I would be there, as an adult, to help her. This may sound like 'mumbo jumbo' but it helped me immeasurably, and I would not be where I am today without Rebecca's help. Obviously, Rebecca would not advocate me smashing Melissa's head in like a pumpkin, but all the good stuff that came before that was due to Rebecca and her expertise. She is an amazing woman and counsellor.

***

Strangely, throughout this period, Frank was still saying that he loved me. Admittedly, in that cliched way people do in films.

'I love you as a person, not as a wife', and 'it is not you, it is me'. It is important that you remember this, as we will be coming back to it later. Bear with me, it will soon have some relevance. Most of the time, though, he treated me with utter contempt. I have never felt so worthless or unloved. In one instance, I came downstairs after he came home after one of his nights out and my breast fell out of my dressing gown (and it was the good one!). Well, he looked at me with utter disgust, and said quite aggressively, "Have some self-respect and put that away!" I found it *so* hurtful. So, I did what any self-respecting woman would do and grabbed it and wobbled it up and down on purpose in his face…

Sometimes I would deliberately talk about our previous sex life, and he could not bear to hear about it. I do think he was having sex with Melissa by now, so maybe he felt guilty or embarrassed. Perhaps he was trying to pretend that none of it ever happened. There are really no words to describe the absolute desolation and fear that I felt at this time. I was so sad that Frank had moved so far away from me emotionally. I was also unbelievably hurt that, by now, Frank would have shared with his family what was going on with us and that we were splitting up and almost none of them had reached out to me. The only person who did was Danielle, Frank's brother's wife and for her kindness, I am forever grateful.

The impending loss of Frank's family and his children, Tilly and Bradley, caused me deep, emotional pain that I do not think I will ever really recover from. I was hoping that I would be able to maintain a relationship with his parents and children but, sadly, that has not proved to be the case. I genuinely loved all these people, but my intuition, again, told me that I would lose them, not least because I knew that Frank would have told them all that I was crazy. Remember, my own children believed this too and he had convinced me, myself, that I was. This was gaslighting at the highest level, and if there were awards for it, he would be grand master. However, I was really shocked when Rebecca pointed out that I was being gaslighted. She gave me a list of the sort of things that gaslighters say, and Frank had said every single one of them to me at some point.

I also knew that Frank had told Nick and Melissa that I was crazy; Nick admitted as much to me months later and apologised for it. All my doubts about Frank and Melissa's relationship would eventually be brought into the light and all my behaviour would be vindicated. It did not stop anything being less painful. I would not have got through this difficult, confusing, and upsetting time without the love and support of friends and family. This brings me on nicely to Donna and Dave, who do not realise how much they helped me and how much I was grateful for their unwavering support.

After I confessed all to Donna and Dave, they could not have done anymore to help me. Dave, especially, as he had previously undergone counselling himself so knew a lot about diverse ways to deal with stress. I wanted to kill Melissa right back then, but Dave managed to dissuade me from completely losing my temper. Melissa was occupying a lot of my thoughts and Dave taught me to imagine putting her 'in the bin' and then putting the lid down. Dave also did a recording of his voice on my phone, saying loudly, "PUT HER IN THE BIN AND NOW PUT DOWN THE LID!" I listened to this when I needed bringing back down to earth. Psychologically, this does work, for a time, at least. I am sorry to Dave that I could not make it stick long-term and ended up killing her anyway.

During the day I was able to supress the thought that Frank and I would no longer be together, but at night the thoughts of our inevitable separation consumed me. Night after night, Frank was able to sleep soundly like a baby and his snores penetrated the wall between us. My husband was sleeping in our bedroom and in our bed. Sometimes, in the night, I would go and wake him so that he could see my distress. I wanted him to feel the same distress that I felt, but I was met with stern rebukes. 'Go to sleep!', 'I am tired!', 'what is this achieving!' This would just make me sob even harder, until I had to run to the bathroom to throw up.

Half of me loved Frank and half of me hated him, in equal measure. He was watching me go mad with grief and he did not, or could not, help me stop. At times, I know that I behaved like a wailing banshee, but he showed me no emotion at all. Nothing. Our marriage was collapsing before our very eyes and I was trying to hold on to it with everything that I had, but Frank was able and willing to let it crumble and decay into the earth. At this point, I was unable to picture my life without Frank in it. I had really given it my all, until I was spent and emotionally ruined.

I used to think, *He would not do that to me, no way.* I knew that he could not mean what he was doing to me. I had thought that we had loved each other so much. I could not see any future at all. I wondered when the impact of what was happening would start to lessen. I wondered how long it would be before I fully accepted that Frank did not want to be with me; when I would have certainty of that. But for now, it just felt like a huge explosion of pain that happened in my mind at random moments. In bed at night, all I could feel was deep and painful loss.

I thought if we could just get back to how things were, then I would do everything differently. If I could just remove my heart and stop it from hurting. I knew that I loved him too much. When you build your life around a person and their family and their children and then that person that you thought you knew ceases to exist, all you are left with is an empty cavity in the centre of your soul. You are plunged into a black sea where nothing exists except you and your pain.

Frank started to be horrible to me. He talked to me like I was something one of the cats sicked up. I do not know what I had done to deserve this. My nanna always said that there was a very thin line between love and hate, and I had never really understood it, until now. I would beg and plead with him to try to at least talk to me like I was some part human, but it was not happening. I could not stand the cruelty. I told him that as he was the one who wanted our marriage to end then he should move out, but he refused to leave, preferring instead to make every minute of me living in our marital home sheer hell on earth.

Quite often I would walk the streets rather than being in the house with him. I would turn up on various friends' doorsteps asking if I could stay. Frank never questioned if I was okay, or where I was going. By now, I do not think he would have cared if I had been murdered myself. Unbelievably, throughout this time, I continued with all my usual wifely duties; washing, ironing, cleaning, and cooking us both a meal every evening. Out of everything that has happened, and since I have learned the full truth, I cannot believe that Frank let me continue doing all of this when all the time he was throwing his cocktail sausage down Melissa's bowling alley. Please excuse me for being so common.

Chapter 17

Last June was an extremely difficult and challenging time. I told Frank that he had ruined my life and left me heartbroken and *he* had the nerve to be offended. I really loved him and his family and found it so hard to come to terms with. I hoped that I had treated Tilly and Bradley like my own, because I certainly loved them like they were my own. I had given them my all and had tried to be the best stepparent that I could be but, at the end of the day, it counted for nothing. Also, Frank's mum and dad; I had tried to be a good daughter-in-law, but all I now took from this was that I had fallen short. I had failed.

One evening in June, Frank and I had one of the best evenings we had had for a long time. Frank seemed more like his 'normal' self. I was lulled into a false sense of security and held out renewed hope that we could turn this around. He was being nice, so I just decided to go with it. He had run out of alcohol, so maybe that was why? We watched television together and it just felt like old times. No wonder, again, that I felt so confused. We talked about us not being together anymore in quite a calm and rational way. He said that he would miss me! He had suffered a nasty fall in the shed that evening – had he had a blow to the head? I wanted to cuddle him, even though I do not 'do blood' but it did not feel appropriate. I told him that I no longer knew what to do in this type of situation. I was so confused.

The very next night he reverted to type and was adamant that we sort out our mobile phones, as both were in my name.

I had to ring our provider and ask them to separate them. I was so choked-up that I could hardly talk. I gave them permission to deal with Frank. It felt a bit surreal that my life had come to this place where things were beginning to become wrenched in two. After the call, I sobbed uncontrollably. Frank did not even look at me, put an arm around me or offer any form of comfort. He played *Wooduko*.

The following morning, after knowing that I had an exceedingly difficult previous evening, Frank informed me before he left for work that he would be going to Melissa and Nick's that evening to 'have a laugh'. He wondered why I was put out. I thought, *Are you having a laugh?* Your 18-year relationship is ending, and you are going round to the house of the woman who has caused our break-up, to have a laugh? I am not going to lie, I was pissed. I contacted my close friend, Debbie, to go out with her that same evening, with the intention of getting drunk as it felt like it was the only way that I was going to deal with him being there with her.

I had moments of great strength and a feeling that I would get through this, followed by a crushing sense of self-doubt. At this time, my mood could turn on a pin head, depending on the circumstances. Throughout it all, I had such a sensation of intense grief for the loss of the Frank, the one that I had thought I had known so well, that it caused physical pain in my soul. I never want to feel this again. It is quite sad that Frank has ruined any further relationship for me, because if I were to let my guard down again and history repeated itself... Well, I am telling you now, I cannot do it.

In the hope of igniting some sort of feelings for me, I instructed an estate agent to come around and value our house. I purposely timed it so that he would still be there when Frank came home from work. He looked mildly surprised when he got home and I introduced them to each other, but he was not heartbroken like I had expected. In fact, I do not think if I had inserted a hand grenade up Frank's arse and it had gone off that he would have changed his facial expression. I realised quite quickly that I had ballsed-up. He did not give a toss. But, at this point, I did not know what his real plans were. If I had, it would have made more sense.

***

It had only taken one viewing of our house for us to fall in love with it. We both loved it on our first viewing. It was Victorian, which is admittedly my favourite style of house, but Frank had loved it as much as I did. To be honest, we did not really need a second viewing, as I knew intuitively that this was where we were going to make our home. It had two large bedrooms, to accommodate all the children, and Frank and I shared the little room whilst Tilly and Bradley were still coming at the weekends. We had a huge garden. It was idyllic in every way. I have never been as happy as I was in that house, when the six of us were all there together. Leaving it would be a huge wrench – for me, at least.

When I got upset about leaving our home, Frank belittled my feelings by saying that he had just bought the house because *I* liked it. This was about as far from the truth as one could possibly get. When I would get upset about leaving, he kept saying, "It is just a house." I asked him to move out then, but he kept saying that he had nowhere to go. I suggested that he go and live with his parents until the house had sold, but he complained that it was too far for him to drive to and from work each day. Nobody should be subjected to living with somebody who makes their life a misery, if the other person is the one who wants to end the marriage.

After a particularly difficult few days, I suggested to Frank that he move in with Melissa and Nick. I thought it would be easier all round. He wanted to spend every waking moment with them anyway, and he and Melissa worked together so they would be able to leave for work at the same time. He thought that my suggestion was ludicrous, but I thought that it made perfect sense. He refused to ask them, so I told him that I would ring Melissa on his behalf. The conversation went something like this:

Me: "Hello, Melissa, it is me. I was wondering, as you are such good friends with Frank, if it would be possible for him to come and stay at your house? You have plenty of room and things are very toxic between us, now."

The response I had was from 'screechy' Melissa, the one I had heard previously in the street, when I was with my friend, Lin.

Melissa: "Why should Frank move out, he pays the mortgage!"

From where had she got this information? Cleary Frank had told her this. So, my wages did not contribute to it at all then? I lost my shit. I told her to just, "GO AWAY AND FUCK OFF!"

I passed the phone to Frank, and he said to *her*, "I am sorry about that."

What on actual earth? I told him not to apologise to her on my account, and then she started crying. I actually heard her say,

"After everything she has put me through!" What the actual fuck? Was this some kind of joke? I had not smoked for eight years, but afterward I demanded that Frank rolled me one or I was in serious jeopardy of going around there and killing her there and then.

We were not happy with the estimated value that the first estate agent gave us, so I rang another one and arranged for her to come around. I had sought some legal advice and they had told me to take charge of the selling of the property, as then they would deal directly with me. I did not even want this to be happening, so I did not feel that I owed Frank any favours. I will always remember when Kellie turned up on my doorstep to do the viewing. Firstly, she was petite and beautiful. I warmed to her instantly. Also, she really loved the house, which was another plus. She asked me why 'we' were moving, and I told her that my husband was leaving me. Or, rather, that he did not want to be with me, but that he would not leave.

Well, she was warm and kind and said that I would get through this, and then proceeded to tell me that her husband had left her the previous year with two small children, so we both ended up crying, which, truly, could only happen to me! It was like a mutual counselling session. I remember thinking that her husband must be a grade A arse as she was slim, pretty and had a lovely personality. Was he mental? I had not met him, but decided he must be clinically insane. When she left, I cried my eyes out and tortured myself with thoughts and memories of all the happy times we had shared in the house. Particularly Christmas and us all playing games together. Not to mention all the work I had put into decorating it for the past year.

When Frank came home from work, I was still an emotional mess. I was still crying and my eyes were like pissholes in the snow. There was no love, no support, no sympathy, no *feelings*. I did not know where he had gone again; I still do not know where he went. I guess it must have been straight into Melissa's knickers. I was pleading with God on my knees to tell me where Frank had gone. The past 18 years of my life seemed irrelevant. It was like I no longer counted in Frank or any of his family's lives. It was a very desolate and lonely place to be.

I talked to myself constantly; telling myself that I would need to move on. I wondered if I would be able to pretend that this period of my life had never even happened. It felt as though it had all been a lie. Our wonderful love story, our marriage, my relationships with his family and with his children. Had it all been a lie? I certainly felt that, collectively, they had all broken me. I felt like I had been 'had' in some sort of twisted joke. Apart from these thoughts, at the back of my mind was the constant thought, *Where am I going to live? And what am I going to do?* I was living in terror. I thought I could not be by myself; I knew I did not like the dark. What if somebody breaks in when I am at home alone? These thoughts were all-consuming. I had to pray for help. I could not do this alone.

The night after Kellie had been round, Frank went to Melissa and Nick's to 'play pool' – for five and a half hours! I mean, you must be thinking by now that I am the most gullible fool that you have ever read about. Not for the first time, I waited for him, out in the rain, to come home. You must understand, I was terribly lonely, and I think having some sort of breakdown. I found a good hiding place where I could wait around the corner for him and he would not see me. It was so hard not to resent Melissa and Frank for ruining my marriage and my happy life. The whole scenario felt ridiculous. Frank told me that he was ending our marriage based upon our arguing, failing to acknowledge that it had been caused by his over-familiarity with not one, but with two women. Yet he still managed to blame me.

His mood was infinitely worse on the days where he spent a full day with Melissa. On those days he would come home being nasty and spiteful. I imagined her really winding him up into this state. He, talking about how horrible I was and she, agreeing and saying that the poor little lamb should not have to suffer like this. And he would look down forlornly and then she would give his hand a reassuring squeeze, or she would touch his leg and his little loins were stirred into life. It was like he took on board all her nasty traits. At the end of our relationship and when I found out what I found out, I could not work out where one of them begun and the other one ended.

Chapter 18

Although I did not want to, I got myself some legal advice. Anything pertaining to us splitting up made me terribly upset and anxious and I did not want to do it. It seemed that the more upset I got, the more Frank enjoyed it. He would wait until I was feeling low and throw in a comment about 'sorting out the finances', or start talking about 'when we leave the house', or 'things we need to do'. I could tell that he was also getting advice from his dad (as he is good with figures), and this really hurt. Also from Melissa, as Frank seemed to know what forms we needed to fill in and, as Melissa had a lot of experience in the field of divorce, I knew that she was helping him. Frank would not have had a clue.

I continued my counselling with Rebecca, and she was a real lifeline at these times. She really seemed to 'get' me. Clearly Frank did not, or did he? Or he just did not care? As was usual, my friends were fantastic. They checked in on me regularly, thought about me, and some prayed for me, depending on their religious persuasion. I must also mention my cousin, Alison; she was always on the end of a phone, despite living in the states, and was never shy at saying it exactly as it was. Frank should think himself lucky; if he had been living with her in the last few months, he would not have any clothes as I know that she would have cut them all up with some very sharp scissors, and all his worldly belongings would have been chucked out of the window onto the street. She suggested that I hire a private detective but, in my gut, I knew that Frank and Melissa were fornicating anyway.

One night, Frank was invited to dinner at his mum and dad's, and he had said that I could go too. *This is a bit weird*, I thought. Frank's niece was over from Canada with her boyfriend. I would have loved to have seen them and I really wanted Frank's parents to help us, so I was going to go. That is until Frank said to me that I could go on the proviso that I did not mention anything at all to do with us splitting up and that I must 'act normally' and say nothing. How did I allow myself to be dictated to like this? So I ended up not going as one thing is for sure, I cannot keep quiet in the middle of a crisis, or at any other time. I was incredibly sad that I would never see Frank's niece ever again, though, or his parents.

After me strongly resisting doing anything about the finances, Frank ground me down. We agreed that we would now need to put the house on the market, and we decided to do that with Kellie. My solicitor had told me that with a fight I could get more out of the sale of the house, as Frank was earning four times as much as I did, and I had run the home, which had enabled him to work. Frank seemed to want to sort things out fairly but, for some reason, people cannot seem to help turning nasty once it is all over. I also knew that, by now, he was getting help from his daughter, Tilly, who was a mortgage broker and a financial advisor. Again, I found this painful. I loved her and could not believe how readily people were able to put the boot in. I am pleased, though, that I came through this without any advice or financial help, from anyone, but I did wonder why none of Frank's family, who claimed to love me, would reach out to me and see if I were okay.

Frank even took Tilly and Bradley out for a meal, which was something that he had never done in 18 years. I so wished for someone to stab me to death and put me out of my misery.

I constantly wished that I had the balls to commit suicide and that it was not a sin. It hurt even more when Frank came back from the meal and said that Tilly and Bradley had not even asked after me. I just kept saying to him, "And another 40 lashes," and he would roll his eyes. I hope that I never again allow anyone to treat me so badly. I will proceed through the rest of my life with extreme caution, and I suggest that you do the same. I would never in a million years have expected this to go so very wrong. And I will never understand why Frank felt it necessary to be so cruel to me.

The next item on the agenda was divorce. At first, Frank claimed that he did not want a divorce, as he had no intention of ever remarrying. As he has said that, I am fully expecting the opposite to be true because every word that comes out of that man's mouth has turned out to be a lie. But he cannot marry Melissa now, as I have killed her. Ha! I said that I was not prepared to stay married to somebody who did not want to be with me and though I have no intention of *ever* getting married again myself, I said, "What if I want to get remarried?" It was in the vain hope that he would fall into my arms and realise how wonderful I am (you have guessed right – that did not happen).

So, I went berserk! I emptied our box of paperwork on the floor like a frenzied mad woman, looking for our marriage certificate. I was hysterical. The whole thing broke my heart with no emotion again from this new robot, Frank. Getting divorced online, by the way, is as easy as ABC. You do not even need to give a proper reason, it just says 'marriage irretrievably broken down'. It takes a matter of minutes. At my time of writing, it costs £600. I was annoyed because I really yearned to name Melissa in the divorce proceedings, but it would have cost so much more if we had used solicitors that I did not think that she was worth it. She knew, Frank knew, and I knew, that the major reason for our marriage breakdown was *her* and one day she would be made to face the consequences.

I could not resist taking a screenshot of the divorce application, so that Frank could show it to her. I envisaged them laughing about it together and her swishing her unbrushed hair about. I expect that he did show her as they shared everything, including bodily fluids, as it transpires. The next day Kellie came to do a floor plan of the house. She was very professional, even though I could tell that she was not exactly Frank's major supporter. Frank had taken the day off because it was sunny, so was hanging around whilst Kellie was taking photos. She could tell how much I was suffering. When she left, I had another breakdown. I was constantly swinging through all the stages of grief and it was so, so tiring.

I also felt incredibly guilty. I thought (I still do) that I must be the worst mother in the world for putting my poor children through this again. I hate him for what he has done to James and Rosie; had they not had enough hurt and pain in their lives? I was back to feeling suicidal again now but could not go through with it. I did fantasize about different methods, but was sadly lacking in the bravery department. Not only that, but I had children, family and friends who would have been heartbroken, even if Frank and his family would not have been. I quite often sobbed on Patrick and Diana, the friends who lived next-door-but-one to Nick and Melissa. Not having a dad, it was lovely to just get a cuddle from Patrick who was like a father figure. They, like everyone else, could not believe that this was happening. Poor Diana kept saying, "But you and Frank are such a lovely couple!"

I could not sleep through worrying about the house selling. When I could not sleep, I used to lie listening to Frank's snoring in the bedroom next door and I was constantly amazed that he seemed not to have a care in the world. I kept thinking about all the good times we had in the house, even funny times, like the time that my daughter threw her knickers across her bedroom and they had landed on her bedside table lamp and caught fire. She slept through smoke billowing throughout her bedroom, whilst the rest of us were downstairs. It was fortunate that James and I had smelt smoke and that nobody was hurt. The house stank of burning for days.

When I told our next-door neighbours, Liz and Neil, that Frank and I were splitting up Liz cried, and I cried. We had become quite close over the years and Liz had always looked after the cats when we went on holiday. She said that she would really miss us and the cats. It was really upsetting. I told Frank when he came home from work that I had told Liz and that she was upset and, again, there was no emotion from him. It was so weird. I did not know at this point if there was anything that would cause him to show or feel any emotional response. He was drinking heavily, so I do not know if this was the cause. I wonder if he is upset that Melissa is dead, or if he will just look for a new wife?

***

It was tedious work keeping the house clean and tidy all the time for viewings. Bearing in mind that I loved our house and did not want to leave it. If I had wanted to sell it and to leave then it would have not felt so awful, I am sure. It was a weird situation, as I swung from enjoying still being in the house, and then wanting it all to be over so that the mental cruelty would stop and I would finally have some peace. During this time, Frank and I got along reasonably well, for the most part. We still ate meals together and would watch television. If one of the children phoned to talk to me, they were understandably perplexed if I said we were watching a programme and eating dinner. A lot of people could not understand how I was still cooking for him, or even that we sat in the same room, but I still loved him and wanted to be with him.

When we did argue, I would point out that we had never had a cross word throughout the whole of our marriage, which was true – until Melissa came into our lives. When I said this he would become angry as he could not cope with any criticism of her at all. He would then wonder why I, and some other people, thought that they must be having an affair. One day, I noticed that the Viagra had gone missing from his bedside drawer. I knew that he had not used it on me! When I questioned it, he said that he had 'suddenly noticed' that it had become out of date. Yes, okay, and the earth is flat.

Despite everything that was going on, Frank still was claiming to love me. He just 'didn't love me like that' and he 'couldn't give me what I needed'. All I really needed was him to get back to 'normal' and stop thinking he was some kind of lothario, with loads of women after him! I was desperate to talk to Nick. I used to pray that I would bump into him. I really wanted his take on all that was going on. Donna very kindly came with me to have a look at a flat. It did not turn out to be suitable, but I obviously needed to find somewhere to live. But even at this late stage, I still thought that Frank would come to his senses.

Frank's drinking had escalated to an alarming level now. I still do not know how he never got arrested for drink driving.

One evening he went to Melissa and Nick's until one o'clock in the morning. When he came home, he was drunk and feisty. We almost had a punch-up as I tried to push him out of the back door, whilst he was trying to get in. I wish I were a bit stronger because he won, which I found very disappointing. That night, he continued drinking all night.

While Frank had been out during the evening, I decided to go and visit my friend, Dave H, and his wife, Lesley. I met Dave H through work and, over time, we became friends. His wife, Lesley, was a wise and beautiful person. I told them both what was going on. Dave used to be a teacher and before I even offered my view on Frank, he said that he always thought that Frank might be autistic, or certainly on the spectrum. They both suggested that he had become obsessed with Melissa and that he could not help it. I also told them about his excessive drinking and they said that alcohol can change people's personalities. I was aware of this, but it did help hearing somebody else say it.

Apart from everything else, they were mostly extremely shocked. They, like so many others, thought that our relationship was rock-solid. And, like others, agreed that it did not really make any sense. Out of everything that has happened, both during, and since, I still do not understand what happened. Bearing in mind that Frank and I never, ever, had a cross word throughout our entire marriage, until Melissa came along. And Frank knew that I loved him more than anybody else ever would. Why would you throw that away?

Frank now had bowel problems too. He was spending an inordinate amount of time in the loo. I was really worried about him. I offered to make him an GP appointment, but he refused to have one. I did think that he was not finding this all as easy as he was portraying. He spent a lot of time talking to Tilly and she did not even mention me now. I clearly had never really existed in their lives but, at this point, I was beginning to feel beyond hurt. He invited Bradley over for Sunday lunch but, again, informed me that I had to act normally and mention nothing. I cannot believe that I went along with his demands! I loved Bradley too, so when he left, I was distraught, wondering if I would ever see him again. Frank ignored me, picked up his book and lay in the sun reading.

Rebecca continued to help me through everything. My children were really supportive now that they fully realised what Frank had been doing to me. They had honestly been brainwashed by Frank, telling them that it was my fault. I was so grateful for everybody's support. My friend, Leigh, kept sending me messages to cheer me up and my friend, Robert (he one that I may have had a teenage dalliance with), and another friend, Deano, also kept checking in on me, bless them.

Melissa had completely derailed our lives. You cannot account for the Melissas of this world. I am sure that she is not the only one of her ilk. However tightly I tried to hold on to Frank, she would be there trying to come between us. People like her take pleasure in striding into your world and taking what they want from it. I doubt that she looked back to see what she had done or what she had taken from us. I hope that, one day, Frank will truly understand what Melissa was capable of. I do remember at one point asking him to ask her if she had dabbled in witchcraft. She certainly had a very unnatural hold over him; she had become like a Frank-magnet.

On 21st July last year, the house sold for the first time. Kellie had phoned me about five minutes before Frank came home from work for lunch to tell me. I felt like my entire innards had been ripped out. I could not resist giving Frank a fake, "Congratulations!" I am nothing if not sarcastic. I told him that I was going out to try to process the information. He said that was good as he was going back to work early to take Melissa shopping in Tesco! Really? What? If it had not been so callous or evil, I would have laughed. She had her own car that she was perfectly capable of driving, she had plenty of time to go shopping in between shifts, and, most importantly, she *had her own husband!* I wish that they had told me that they were having an affair at this point, as then the whole thing would have made more sense.

I was dying to talk to Nick. All my friends also wanted to know how he felt about everything. Did he know about the time that Frank and Melissa were seen having a coffee in McDonald's car park? Did he know about the 'shopping'? Did he know that the very next day after shopping, Frank picked Melissa up early again so that they could go to collect his new taxi plate? Was that even true? I now wonder if these early pick-ups were so that they could go somewhere for sex. Were they having sex in Melissa's marital home, while Nick was out? I was still puzzled about the mysteriously disappearing Viagra tablets…

When Frank was feeling particularly vindictive, like when I had stopped crying for a brief interlude, he would bring me crashing back down to earth, by stating in a very harsh voice, "Why have you not had anything back about the divorce yet?" He took real comfort from my feeling very vulnerable. I swear to you, he was nothing at all like this, until he met *her.* I kept asking him what his plans were. He continuously claimed that he did not have any. I did not believe it. Frank is the sort of person to do a list for the most mundane of tasks; he would not 'wing his way through' like I would, without a plan. To think I felt sorry for him at the thought of him sitting alone in his flat with no one. There is no fool like and old fool.

And so, the weeks went by. Every weekend he went to Nick and Melissa's. I would go out with my friend, Debbie. She was, and has been, incredibly supportive. Leigh, again, proved to be an immeasurable support. During last year's summer holidays, I went on a visit to my hometown, to see all my old friends. Just before I left, the house sale fell through. I was pleased, and I had a wonderful time in Watford. All the crowd were so lovely to me. Laura (Alan's sister), was amazing. Alan even gave me a lift to my friend Fiona's, which was a little strange, though I had long forgiven him for leaving me. I need to mention my friend Fiona's triplets, they are such a credit to her and her husband, Brenig. Their daughter, Grace, sang in front of me, and she has a voice like an angel. Robert and Deano had driven all the way from Watford to Plymouth to take me back to Watford when I stayed at Laura's.

When I got home, Frank immediately started on me, talking about changing bank accounts and me opening my own account. I gave him a hug on my return, as I usually would, and it was like hugging an ice sculpture. Now I know what I know, he must have felt awkward, as it had only been a few hours prior to that when I suspect he had been lying naked somewhere with Melissa. He kept saying in an exasperated tone, "Nothing is moving forward." I found it all so hard, so cold and so cruel. I really could not believe that this was all coming just from him. He would also shout, "WE'RE SPLITTING UP!" Did he not think that I might have realised that?

Chapter 19

The next thing that happened was somewhat unusual. I was casually walking down the street one day when I felt something 'give'. I honestly thought that my insides were falling out. It was more than a little alarming and despite everything else that was going on, I thought that I had better go to the doctor, whereupon another interesting thing happened. I saw a nurse practitioner; she was lovely, and we bonded immediately. I must add that this was *after* my embarrassing internal examination. In conclusion, she stated that my uterus had 'fallen down'. She said that with some 'help' from my partner, this could be temporarily rectified. I told her that my partner was leaving me, aside from the fact that we had not been intimate for ten years, so I had been living like a nun. She agreed that I had a bit of a problem then.

She could not understand why I should have a prolapsed uterus as she said it usually happened to overweight ladies, and she had never heard of anybody being aware of their uterus falling down either. I told her that she had better do another examination, this time of my stomach! She told me that her husband had informed her that he was having an affair in front of their ten-year-old daughter, and while she was cooking the dinner. She said that she knew that he had told her deliberately in front of their daughter in the hope that she would not overreact. So, she took the saucepan that she had been cooking with and smashed him around the head with it! She said there was blood everywhere and that he called the police, but he decided not press charges, as she had been 'provoked'.

I said, "Was it worth it?"

She said, "Oh yes, definitely!"

This was the second woman I had seen lately whose husband had left them. There was a theme going on. First Kellie and then her. Again, I looked at her; she was incredibly attractive, she was smart, and she was funny. Not for the first time, I wondered what was wrong with men and do they always think that the grass is going to be greener? I was not too worried about my uterus falling out. As far as I know it still is. In fact, I welcomed it, because alongside my lob-sided breast, at least I would be very unattractive to all men now, and safe from any further hurt. Can you imagine saying, "OK, I can have sex with you, but excuse my wonky breast and while you are down there, please would you push my insides back in? Thank you."

Aside from Kellie's husband leaving her and the nurse practitioner's husband leaving her, I also had to go and see the nurse at the surgery. It was becoming unbelievable – her husband had just left her too! Then, I went to have my nails done and, you have guessed it, her husband had left her! I remember thinking that there must be something in the air making this happen all around me. The final one was when I came to rent the house that I am now living in. It became available because the tenants had split up and the man had left his partner!

I am currently not a fan of men in general. I had trust issues before, but now they are in such a heightened state that is going to take somebody amazing to alter my mindset. My friend, Diane, says, "Men are disgusting creatures!" And I quite agree.

My friend, Terry, who is male, says, "When will you women realise that all men are c***ts?"

I have arrived there now, so do not worry. And please do not get me wrong, I still have some incredibly good and special male friends and I even love some of them, but I am not going to let any of them hurt me. I now operate a one strike and you are out policy, which is sad, but let us call it 'safeguarding' of my soul.

**

I have no idea how I managed to remain in the marital home for the last few months before Frank and I finally split. I was still begging him at this stage to move out, but he would not budge. It was undeniably cruel. He now would not sit with me on our sofa, which is where we always sat together to eat our evening meal and to watch television, but, instead, would get down on the floor and sit on the rug with his back to me. I found this extremely painful and it made me feel that I must be so disgusting and awful that he could not bear to be near me or to look at me. I did not contemplate that he might be feeling guilty. He was still happy to eat the meals that I was cooking for him, though, and we were even still going food shopping together. It was such a crazy existence.

I spent at least 90 per cent of my life crying. I was at one point going to live at Donna and Dave's; they were always offering me a place to stay. My friend, Diane, had even said that I could stay at her house, and we had not even known each other that long. I am quite stubborn, so even though Frank was making my life a complete misery, I still thought, *Why should I be the one to leave?* I had also been advised against it by my solicitor. I could not equate what was going on at this time with my kind, loving, and warm husband, with whom, in the past, I had been so intimate.

In August I went to visit James and Sophia again. Frank was so excited about me going – he loved me going away. He would always say, "How long are you going for?" I did not think about the fact that this would leave him free to see Melissa as much as he could whilst I was gone. I suppose, at the time, I did not fully believe that they were having an affair. I still had this tiny voice in my head that was saying, *No, he would never hurt you like that*. I must question my sanity at this time, and where was my intuition that I usually relied on so very much?

I also remember crying to Rebecca, saying that I was worried about Frank living by himself and being lonely and drinking himself into an early grave. I even convinced myself that it was possible that he might die. If only he had thought about me half as much as I had thought about him. As usual, I had a lovely time at James and Sophia's. And while I was there, they told me the joyous news that Sophia was pregnant. I was ecstatic. It had given me something positive to think about and I was over the moon! I made a pact with myself right then that I would not contemplate suicide again, ever, even if I were mentally on my knees, because I was going to be a grandma and that was more important to me than anything.

Unfortunately, I was not able to share the news with anybody else as the news was very early, but I liked nursing this secret and every time I thought about it, I had a warm feeling of happiness in my heart. When I was diagnosed with breast cancer, I asked God to keep me alive long enough to meet my grandchildren and now we were there, part way along this road. I did find it sad that Frank would not be able to play any part in his grandfather role, but it really is his loss. My granddaughter is here, as I write, and she is amazing and he is missing out massively. I do hope that some dirty sex with Melissa brought you as much joy as my granddaughter is bringing to my life, but I doubt it.

Frank's birthday was the following month, in September. What are you supposed to do if you live in the same house, do some things together, but not all, you still love the person, but they look at you like you are something the cat dragged in? I decided to make him a photograph album of our life together. Nobody on earth knows that I did this, until now... Friends warned me not to do anything for his birthday, but I have never been particularly good with authority. I printed out loads of photographs of everything that we had done together, from our wedding to our holidays, to family events, to all six of us being together. I also wrote him a card in which I wrote how sad I was that this would be the last birthday that we would ever celebrate together.

Oh yes, I can be quite cruel too! I hope it hurt him as much as it hurt me writing it. Anyway, I presented it to him, and he looked suitably upset; I do not understand why considering what he was doing. He read it all. I had also scanned love letters we had written to each other and put them in there. He looked like he was going to cry and then he went to the bathroom, like he did now that he had this bowel problem. I wonder if he was counting the cost of what he was throwing away? I am sure Melissa was good in the sack, but was she worth giving up 18 years, our family life, and our home for? I really hope that she had been worth it and if she was *that* good in the sack, then well done her!

I told Frank about my insides falling out, but he did not care. He did not care about anything at all now, except Melissa.

Sometimes, I would catch him in the kitchen, just staring out of the window. It looked like he was contemplating things, but he never looked very happy when he was doing this. I will never know if he was thinking about me, or us, or if he was simply thinking about Melissa and wishing that he were with her. It was hard not to feel really rubbish about myself. I did not understand what I had done wrong because I could not have tried any harder to be a good wife and he knew that I would have laid down my life for him.

***

Before I went to James and Sophia's, I wrote a lot of letters. Firstly, I wrote to Frank's children, Tilly and Bradley. I apologised to them for breaking up their family when their dad and I got together. I told them how much I loved their dad and that this was not what I wanted. I said that I hoped that they would have happy memories of our family lives together and I told them that I loved them and that I always would.

I also wrote to Sharon, Frank's ex-wife, asking her to forgive me for my part in what had happened and I wrote to Tom and apologised to him for hurting him when I left him and now I realise how painful it must have been, because now I *really* understood it. I could also fully understand now why he was so angry at that time, because I have been incredibly angry, and, as it turns out, he is a better person than I am, because I have felt so angry that I have killed someone.

I also wrote to my ex-mother-in-law and apologised for hurting her son. I did not expect to achieve anything out of this, apart from letting these people know that I was deeply sorry. If there is such a thing as karma, then my actions have caused me to have the same thing done to me and frankly, karma *is* a bitch. The irony is not wasted on me, that I am responsible for treating other people badly and now look at what has happened. Frank did not understand why I wrote all these letters, saying to me that, "They're all over it now, it's in the past." Well, going on my own feelings, I will never be over this. And his karma is going to be the fact that Melissa is dead.

Chapter 20

I only got one response from my letters, and that was from my ex-mother-in-law, and she could not have been more kind. She was also shocked that this had happened as she thought that Frank and I were strong. She said that I did not deserve what had happened to me, which was lovely of her, but that is open for debate. I am so sad that Tilly and Bradley did not answer. I honestly could not have done any more to try to be a good stepmother.

Our house eventually sold, after a lot of toing and froing. I was devastated due to my love of the house, but also relieved as my suffering was soon to be ending. What did drive me bonkers was the fact that as I was dealing with the estate agent. I would pass the information onto Frank and because *he* had now become such a prolific liar, he would not believe anything I said, so then he would ring them to clarify what I had told him. I had to phone Kellie to apologise because he even started to get on her nerves. But we now both had to find somewhere to live.

Frank became even more secretive than I thought was possible. There were many 'secret' telephone conversations, people would see him out walking and he would always be on his phone. There were more muffled voices coming from his workshop and he started taking his phone right up to the end of our garden, or would sit at the bar, so I could not hear him. I liked to keep one step ahead of him on purpose, because it was the only pleasure I could get. He was seen viewing a house locally and I got told, as I know so many people, and then I would ask him how his viewing went at that address, and he would get really annoyed.

I also phoned several letting agents to find out what houses or flats he was looking at. Oh, I am good at finding things out, and I also kept an eye on places I knew he would look at. Remember that I had known him for 18 years, so knew how his brain worked. I saw a flat that I felt sure he would be interested in; it was out of the immediate area and the rent was reasonable. I phoned and asked them if I could view it and they told me that they had somebody coming to view it that day, and my intuition kicked in and I *knew* it was him. However, I could see that this property would only allow one cat and I wondered which one he would choose to take and why.

Meanwhile, I started to look for somewhere to live too and I eventually found a sweet little house with a garden and a shed and one would allow me to keep all the cats. I told Frank that I would be keeping *all* the cats, and he did not like it, but he was the one that wanted to do this, so, quite frankly, I thought, *well, life is tough sometimes*. He agreed that he would pay half of their upkeep, which would be for their food, cat litter, vet bills, etcetera. He also said that he would drive me to the vets, as I did not have transport, and I said that he was welcome to visit them as they were still his cats too. I maintained saying that throughout, but it never happened. Maybe he was not allowed.

Before I found out for sure that he and Melissa were having sex, I would love to have been able to have maintained a friendship with him. I know that might seem a little strange, but I had looked upon Frank as my best friend and he had said that I was his too. I am sure that Melissa must have put the kibosh on that; perhaps she thought that Frank would come over and that I would try to seduce him, because that is what she would do. But I do have some self-respect left, even if it is only very miniscule.

I started in earnest to sort out all my earthly possessions, which I placed in the dining room for ease of moving when the time came. What Frank did not know was that behind the scenes I had been planning my move. I prayed to God that I would be the first one to leave the marital home, because I could not bear the thought of him leaving first and having the pain and emptiness that I knew I would feel. We sorted out who would take what, quite amicably, but I was really hurt when Frank sold all his woodworking equipment and did not even offer me a fiver. He claimed that all the items were bought for him for various Christmas and birthday presents, but he, and I, both know that this was not true.

Knowing how materialistic Melissa was, I did say to Frank several times to look after his money because I knew that she would have no problem spending it for him. I do not know to this day if he listened. I am amazed that I was still being kind and thinking of him, what with all that was going on. He was still maintaining categorically that there was nothing whatsoever going on between them and would say very loudly in my face, "THERE IS NOTHING GOING ON WITH ME AND MELISSA, IT IS ALL IN YOUR HEAD!" And I would feel suitably chastised for not trusting him and thought to myself that I must be a terrible and distrusting person.

I still had not heard from any members of his family, except his sister-in-law, Danielle. I was really annoyed that I had wasted 18 years of my life building these relationships that now counted for nothing. I felt that Frank had been cruel, letting me waste so many years of my life when he could have 'released' me to meet somebody else. I was now 55. Who was going to want a washed-up, twice divorced, menopausal woman with a wonky tit and a prolapsed vagina? I mean, I would not have, if the shoe were on the other foot. Maybe if he had left me when I was 45 I would at least have still had something left going for me.

He had gone off me because I had had cancer. I apologised to him for getting cancer, but pointed out that having cancer had also been a bit of an inconvenient ball ache in my life too. I asked him what he was going to do about my family, particularly my children who had loved him like a dad, and he said that he would keep in touch with them. He also told me that he would phone Trisha, once everything was all over. He has done neither.

I got a date for when I could move into my new home, and I did not tell him. I thought that I would wait until he told me when he was moving out. He came over to me in the kitchen one day, looking very sheepish and said, "I know you do not want to hear this, but I am moving out on the 21st of October."

The bile rose in my throat, but I managed to say, "Well, that is good, then, as I am moving out on the 15th of October."

He did look shocked. I was so thankful that God had answered my prayers and that I was going to be moving out first. I still found it so difficult and upsetting, and at this point felt awful that he, and I (or so I thought), were throwing away an 18-year relationship to sit alone in our separate homes.

***

I asked Frank to be out when I was going to be leaving. I said that I would text him once I was gone. I still wanted him to call it off and was hoping that he would come to his senses. I am nothing if not incredibly stupid. I was so blessed; I had such a lot of help. Dave had a van and offered to move everything for me. I asked some friends to help and they were all amazing. I had help from Leigh, Linda, Mel (who was one of my 'mums' from my school job, but who is now a friend), her daughter, Lottie, Rosie, and Donna, once she had finished work. Because so many hands made light work, the whole thing only took three-and-a-half hours. Once everybody left and I was alone in my house with just the three cats for company, I could not help but have some sort of breakdown, which I can only describe as gut-wrenching sobbing and rocking in a chair wondering how my life had come to this and had turned on its head to such an alarming degree.

I went back to our marital home one more time, once Frank had also moved out, to collect some things that I had not taken previously, and I also informed Frank that I would clean it ready for the new people who were moving in. It was so sad to see our home with its soul ripped out – I could sympathise. It looked so big and so empty. I tried to shut off my thoughts of the happy times and the love that we had all shared there. At least what I had thought was love, anyway. Frank had left a bag of rubbish at the bottom of the stairs and on the top I could see that he had thrown away his Sandals dressing gown from our wedding. This about summed it all up, really. I, too, felt discarded. Now I know what I know, I guess he felt it would be inappropriate to bring that into his new relationship.

Once I had recovered, I made a conscious decision to just get on with it. I had no other choice. There was still crying, for a long time, and I found it particularly difficult when Rosie would come over and would sob on my shoulder, asking me if Frank ever really loved her. At times like this, it was so hard not to kill *him*. I will never forgive either of them for hurting my kids so spectacularly. James had his new life with Sofia in North Yorkshire, but I knew that he was hurting too, and I know that they would both have been concerned about my welfare. They should not have been put in the position where they were forced to worry about me.

I cannot describe enough how grateful I was, and am, for all the support I received. I did not have time to feel lonely as I had a constant supply of visitors and people checking up on me. I was still seeing Rebecca and I would express to her how worried I was about Frank being by himself, not realising that he was far from 'by himself'. If she had doubts about Frank's motives, she never expressed them. She would just sit and listen to me and pass tissues at appropriate moments. Once I settled into my new home, I told her that I did not feel that I needed to see her anymore. I was truly devastated when I left her care. And we did hug at the end, even though that is not the correct etiquette when saying goodbye to your counsellor. When I left her home, for what I thought would be the last time, I sobbed all the way home.

There are other people that I must mention. My Auntie Pam. She has always been there with good advice and kindness. She is not just my auntie, she is one of my best and closest friends. Although disabled and in poor health, she offered to get on a train and come and kick Frank's arse. I know she would have done it if I had let her. My dear friend, Fiona, always on the end of a phone when needed, and she had to listen to me crying a lot. Martyn, my friend from primary and secondary school, who I have known for 51 years, telling me that I deserve better and that someone who deserves me will come along one day. This is kind, but I think that my knight in shining armour has got lost somewhere on the highway. My cousin, Alison, and all my amazing, kind, and loving friends. I am so blessed. And none of these people said that I deserved it because of what I had done to Tom, which they very easily could have done.

My friend Chris, that I used to work with, and her husband, Charles, have been tremendous support. They have invited me out with them, had me around at weekends for lunch and tea, and Charles has done a lot of work in my new house, rubbing down and painting woodwork, aside from the many odd jobs that he has done for me. Leigh too, putting in a cat flap and all the other odd jobs he has helped me with. A special mention to my friend Debbie, who goes out drinking with me, and has put up with my moaning and who has been very patient, when she, or I, only get chatted up by old gentlemen, who would not look out of place in a nursing home.

I cannot reiterate enough how much I loved – love – Frank's children, Tilly and Bradley. It is not difficult to recall special moments that I had with them both. I remember Tilly starting her period when she was staying with us one weekend and I took her to the shops so that she could choose some sanitary products. I explained to her that this was a very important day, as she had become a woman now. I remember another time when she was in a lot of pain with earache and I lay on the bed with her and rubbed her ear in an attempt to make her feel better. You cannot have children every weekend and not forge a bond with them.

I do feel that I took my responsibilities as a stepmother seriously. I know that it can be difficult for children to accept a stepparent, but I did try so hard with them and, as I loved their dad so much, it was not difficult to love them too. Bradley is such a sweet and kind person. I never felt that he resented me, and I am certain that he did love me. It would have been my greatest wish that they would have remained in my life, but obviously I do not know what Frank has told them. I am grateful to Frank's ex-wife, Sharon, that she did say to me once that it was reassuring to her that I was Tilly and Bradley's stepmother, as she knew me and knew that, above all else, I was kind.

Just before Christmas of last year, I did have an email from Tilly, which was less than pleasant and it upset me so much that I immediately deleted it. I responded by saying that I hoped her new stepmother, Melissa, would be better than I was and that I hoped she would find her to be as magnificent as her dad thought she was. Since then, unfortunately, we have had no further contact. I really loved Frank's parents and I did feel at the time that they loved me too but, again, I do not know what Frank has told them. I guess it is the usual nonsense about me being crazy. But, as I have already said, people will only believe what they want to believe.

Chapter 21

I settled well into my new home; I even surprised myself. And I grew to love it. Once I had decorated it and put my own stamp on it, I felt quite happy and secure. It was a small house but it needed it to be so that I did not feel as though I was rattling around in a big space. It was much smaller than my old house so if I did any housework, which did not happen as religiously as it once did, it could be done much more quickly, so it was a win-win, really.

I found it exceedingly difficult to sleep for a long time. I think I must have been running on adrenalin because some nights I did not get more than three hours, and I was still managing to work. My mind would torture me with visions of Frank being all alone and drinking himself into an early grave. He had sold all his tools, used for his woodworking hobby, so I worried that he had nothing to do. He had no friends and although this was not the life that I would have chosen for myself, I did have a lot of company, so I was never alone very much. I felt sorry for him.

By the time I had been in my home for about a month, I started to feel a little happier. I remember feeling surprised at this, and I did not think of Frank every minute of every day. I had truly not expected to feel any happiness ever again. Anyway, it was a bright and sunny Thursday afternoon in November and I was walking home from my local shops when I suddenly noticed Nick walking along the road opposite me. This was the first time that I had seen him since I had moved out and since Frank and I had formally split.

Since I had moved out, I had been dying to bump into him as I wanted to get his views on everything that had gone on. So, I crossed the road to speak to him. November 17th, last year, has got to be up there with one of the worst days of my life. Nick did not give me time to say anything to him first, as he said, "Before you say anything, I think that there is something you should know. Well, Frank and Melissa are together..." I was frozen to the spot. I felt like I had been sucker-punched and that all the air had been expelled from my lungs. It was as though time had stood still.

Up until the very day that I had moved out, Frank had been insisting that there was nothing at all between he and Melissa. And one of his favourite 'get-out-of-jail' cards would be when he would say, "Nick is my best friend, I would never hurt him." Nick now looked like he had seen a ghost. He was pale and sad. To be honest, I would have been less shocked if Nick had smacked me around the face with a wet cod. I had so wanted to believe that Frank would not do this to me, or to us, and now those hopes were destroyed.

My overriding feeling was that I had been an absolute fool. I was especially angry that the pair of them could do this to Nick. What kind of low-life scum were they? Poor Nick. He looked like he was still recovering from the news. I also felt ridiculous. Had I not had enough clues? I could not say a lot, as I was so hurt and devastated. I did remember to ask him if they had convinced him, too, that I was crazy and he confirmed that they had, and he said that he was sorry. We embraced in the street, and I did cry a bit, but I really needed to get away from him and to try to process everything. As soon as I had walked away from him, I regretted not asking him for more details.

Before I walked home, I phoned Debbie and told her, and she drove straight round to comfort me. She and so many of my other friends were angry. She and Elaine sent him a text telling him what they thought of him. How lovely to have friends that will fight your corner! My children were suitably devastated for me, and I must admit that the air was fairly 'blue', with plenty of expletives being used, mostly from me. People could not believe what a lily-livered coward Frank was. I had given him multiple opportunities to tell me the truth but, instead, he had convinced everybody that I was mental. I will never forgive him for this. Who was this man that could do such a thing?

Emotionally, I was right back where I started – before I had started to feel better. I was back into freefall depression, terribly upset and continually crying. I immediately got in touch with Rebecca again and, amazingly, nobody had yet taken my space so I was able to resume seeing her. She was so kind to me. I asked her if she had ever thought that there was something going on with Frank and Melissa and she agreed that some of it might have been explainable, but that she did have 'alarm bells' when I told her about the coffee liaison in McDonald's car park. She said that two married people would not behave so secretively if there was nothing in it. She assured me that I would get through this, even though it seemed daunting and impossible.

Chapter 22

"I'm never getting married," Rosie said, as she did yet more crying on my shoulder. I cannot say that I blamed her at this point. For a moment, I allowed myself to picture it. Frank sitting all alone in his flat, drinking whisky with just his TV for company, and me sitting in mine, feeling terribly isolated and lonely. But now, of course, I knew that this was not the case. He was sitting with *her*. The idea of it created a dull ache in my stomach. I could relive our lives together in my mind – all the times that we sat on the sofa together, usually with our feet up, resting on each other's legs. We would take it in turns in case it became too uncomfortable.

I pictured us lying in bed together, me cuddling into his hairy chest, our legs entwined with our bare feet rubbing together. The invisible cord that bound us together and made us become like one person. That ultimate intimacy of knowing each other, body and soul. My heart broke with every thought, with every moment remembered. Daily, it felt as though a piece of my soul was dying. It was difficult for me to comprehend that there was now another woman sharing the same habits with my husband, whom I knew so intimately. Were they the same, or were they creating their own habits?

You cannot delete a marriage, believe me, I have tried. I have recently bumped into Frank (I will tell you more later), and he seems to think that we should just put the past 18 years behind us and forget that it happened. But my marriage – indeed, both of my marriages – have become a part of who I am.

A divorce cannot negate memories, patterns between a couple, or the traditions within those marriages. They just are. They are just how they will be. Oh, believe me, I would do anything so that I could forget.

I was hurting badly. Even recalling all that has happened brings a lump to my throat and a pain to my heart. Were Frank and Melissa now forging their own memories and traditions? Were they laying together with their bare feet entwined, or touching? Was Melissa now nestling into Frank's hairy chest like I used to? Were they watching TV together, eating their dinner on their laps and discussing what they were watching? Were they going on long walks together? Did they hold hands? Was she content, like I was? Was she telling him that she loved him several times a day, like I did? What sickens me to the core is the thought of her replacing me as a stepmother to Frank's children, or a daughter-in-law to his parents. Am I easily replaceable?

**

When Rosie and I went round to see Nick, (more of which I will explain later), he informed us that Frank and Melissa had not been doing the school run together for some time. Again, this totally floored me. So, Frank had told me even more lies and had been pretending that he was working with Melissa, as usual. I wonder now if they had finished working together because of the nature of their relationship. It is forbidden for a taxi driver to be in a sexual relationship with a school escort, and Frank would have known that if I had found this out, I would have reported it.

It now makes a bit more sense why, when I was walking home one day, I saw Melissa driving a red Lexus. It was the same model as ours, the same colour, and even had the same taxi stickers on it! I nearly swallowed my own tonsils. Obviously, she leered at me when she saw me. I walked through the house and found Frank outside in the garden. I said, "Is there any reason Melissa is driving a car identical to ours, with taxi stickers on it, the same as yours and it's even the same colour?"

He said, nonchalantly, "Yes, she's started taxi driving."

I said, "What about your school run?" And – wait for it – he told me *another* lie and said that they were still doing the school run together, but that she was taxi driving in between.

I was really pissed off. Why did everything they did have to be the same? So, I went back into the house and dressed up as Frank. Wearing his t-shirt, shorts, and trainers. I went outside and showed him. I said, "They say it's flattering if you try to copy other people, ask Melissa. So, I've decided to copy what you're wearing!" I found this hilarious, but it was wasted on Frank. He just raised his eyes heavenward. He did not even laugh (I am nothing if not funny). And so, when Nick told me they had not been working together for some time, I realised that they were really both taxi driving, full-time, for the same company, with the same cars.

I wondered if they had a long-term goal to branch out on their own and set up their own luxury taxi company, seing as the cars are the same, but this never transpired, as far as I know. Certainly, since the break-up, every time I saw his or her red Lexus driving around, great anxiety became triggered in me, and a bit of bile always rose into my throat.

You can imagine my shock and distress when I returned to work after Christmas and I saw Melissa's now familiar red

Lexus in the car park at work! By now, I was getting a taxi into work with a wonderful taxi driver called Stefan. He had just started doing my school run. He was Romanian and, culturally, I really love Romanians. They are helpful and really kind. Bearing in mind I had only just met Stefan. I thought to myself, *surely not?* Surely Melissa would not accept a school run into my place of work? I mean, she knew that I worked there. I started to lose it in the car. Did her cruelty know no bounds? I don't know how I managed not to throw up, but I immediately started crying.

Stefan said to me, "What on earth is the matter?"

I said, "It is the woman my husband has left me for; she is here." I said, "I am so sorry." I remember feeling acutely embarrassed and weak.

He said, "You should not be the one who should feel like this. Anyway, you are much better than her!"

To which I said, "But you do not even know me. I cannot be better than her, otherwise he would still be with me."

He said, "I tell you. I have looked at her four times now and I thought she was a man. She looks like a man." And that was when Stefan became, in my eyes, one of the kindest people I have ever met, and I knew we would be friends.

On Friday afternoons, Stefan's partner, Carmen, used to take me to work. I apologised to her for getting upset in front of Stefan. She said, "She is the one that should be feeling upset and embarrassed, as she is the one who has done this to you. Hold your head up and, besides, I genuinely thought that she was a man." And this is how I came to love *all* Romanians.

However, I did find it terrible to have to look at Melissa, both in the mornings and in the evenings. At first, I tried not to look at her, but when I started to feel a bit better, I did try to front it out. Even so, she acted as though she did not care. Maybe she didn't. And one day she overtly flirted right in front of our car, chatting to yet another taxi driver. She really was shameless.

In March, our divorce came through. I was terribly upset. I know that people may be surprised to read this, especially after what Frank had done to me. But I had gone into our marriage with so much hope for the future. I thought that we would grow old together. Our wedding day played like a video recorder in my mind. I could not shut it off. As soon as I saw the email my stomach lurched. You see, despite everything, I still loved Frank with my whole heart.

I immediately phoned him. I did not even think about it or process it. I could hardly talk. I just said, "As you have seen the divorce has just come through. I did not want this, and I still love you." There was a lot of snotty crying.

Frank did have the good grace to say, "I am sorry."

That morning, over breakfast, or after a 'quickie' before work, of course, Frank would have shared this news with Melissa. So, to add to my abject misery and distress, she got out of her car that morning, leant against it and grinned at me! You can see why she had to die, right?

One time when she was flirting with another taxi driver, I noticed that the bottom of her dark hair was looking much lighter. Like she had attempted to dye it herself. It looked a bit orangey. Remember her hair was deep brown before. I wondered what that was all about, as it looked dry and in terrible condition. Over some weeks, her hair started to get lighter and lighter. I could not believe that not being content with taking my husband, my stepchildren, Frank's family, and my home, she was even prepared to go blonde, so that I could not even enjoy the satisfaction of having my own individual hair colour!

I did ask the question on Facebook. Why she would do this? And the general consensus was that she was trying to be me. Had Frank asked her to dye her hair blonde? Did he want her to look like me? Did she feel insecure because she did not look like me? There were more questions than answers. More things that we will never know or understand. Why in heaven's name would you want to be me? I had lost everything. But I guess there was some poetic justice in the end. She was soon going to lose even more than I had, including her life…

I phoned work in a very distressed state one day and spoke to my line manager about the latest events. Nobody could believe that Melissa would have the gall to take a job where I worked. My work even offered to transfer me but I thought, *why should I be the one to move?* I prayed to God in earnest, to please, please, take her away from me. And he did answer, and one day she was gone as quickly as she had arrived. However, I still felt sick to my stomach if I ever saw one of their Lexuses out and about.

One morning in February, I was out having breakfast with my girlfriends and Frank phoned me. I was shaking when I saw his name come up on the screen. I had seen him that morning on my way to work. He said, "I saw you this morning."

I said, "Yes, I saw you too."

He asked if I was okay. I told him that I was as okay as could be expected. He asked if I had people there. I told him that I was out for breakfast with my friends. He said, "Okay, I'll phone you another time." What was that all about? I have never, ever, found out. At the time, I wondered if he had realised that he had made a terrible mistake.

***

It was exceedingly difficult to feel at all positive leading up to Christmas last year. I had been used to having a full house, with the six of us drinking, having fun, and playing parlour games. This would not necessarily occur on Christmas Day, as usually Tilly and Bradley would spend Christmas Day with Sharon and her new husband. So, quite often, we had our Christmas on Boxing Day or the day after. I used to love the excitement of Christmas, the build-up being even more fun than the actual day. I loved buying and wrapping presents and I was still doing stockings for our 'children' even though they were all grown adults.

On Christmas Eve I decided to go out drinking. I do not know if this was a clever idea, but if a little alcohol was going to take my mind off things, then I thought, *why not?* I met my friend, Di, her partner, Wayne, and their son, McKenzie, in the pub. I used to take McKenzie to and from school the previous year. I do not know what happened but I must have been releasing some sort of pheromones, or else I just looked like a sad single woman who needed rescuing, but I got 'chatted up' by three different men. I was not flattered, as I now think all men think with their genitals only. One of them gave me their phone number on a piece of paper, even though I had made it perfectly clear that I was not interested, but I took it and put it in my bag with no intention of contacting him. Ever.

So last year was hard and emotionally painful for me. I was not even going to decorate the house. It was a tough call to muster up any enthusiasm at all. I think that my good friend, Linda, must have taken pity on me as she came round and presented me with a mini-Christmas tree and a branch with coloured lights on it for me to plug in. I spent Christmas morning by myself and I will confess that I had a little cry and had a bit of a self-satisfying pity party. I wondered if Frank and Melissa were spending their morning together, laughing and opening presents with her wearing a red Mrs Claus see-through negligée.

My ex-sister-in-law picked me up at lunchtime and took me to my stepmum Trisha's. We did all manage to have a lovely day and it was a man-free zone, as all three of us had not got one! It was lovely to spend it with my niece and nephew too, but I was still feeling deeply hurt inside and struggled afresh with the position that Frank had caused me to be in. Boxing Day was okay, as I had Rosie and her new boyfriend, Sammy, with me. But overall, well, I was so relieved when it was all over. I asked Rosie to make sure that she got me a block of Post-it notes for Christmas as I was constantly struggling with all the lies Frank had told me. Rebecca suggested that I wrote them all down and then dispose of them, so that I could put them to bed. In the new year, I did start to write down all of Frank's lies until I was forced to stop. My kitchen began to look like an explosion in a stationery cupboard.

***

This brings me nicely on to Betsy. When Frank first started taxi driving many years ago, he took this elderly lady called Betsy to Exeter to see her ex-husband as he was dying. To cut a long story short, she and Frank became friends, and she took his phone number in case she ever needed a taxi so that she could call him direct. This started off quite simply as a mere acquaintance, but over the years Betsy became more of a permanent fixture in our lives. She definitely had an attachment to Frank.

I do not think that Frank enjoyed the fact that Betsy started to become more and more dependent on him, and I must confess to my instructing him to 'be kind' as she was getting old and did not have any family. As she became increasingly demanding, he would always blame me for telling him to be nice to her, but I did think we might be old one day and we would be grateful if a Good Samaritan were being kind to one of us.

Betsy was also a hypochondriac of the highest order, and she would constantly be putting herself in hospital with various fictitious ailments, usually preferring to do it on high days and holidays. So, we would get phone calls from her saying that she was feeling poorly, at Easter, Christmas and on either her, mine, or Frank's birthday. Many a time we had a phone call from her in the middle of the night. Every time she was in hospital, I would have to escort a nurse into a cleaning cupboard and explain that there was nothing wrong with Betsy and that she was having them on, but they had to treat every admittance as if it were legitimate just in case it ever was.

Betsy also had the local paramedics on speed dial. Anyway, she would be duly carted off to hospital, then we would have to drive to her house, collect her dog, drive to the kennels about an hour away, collect stuff that she might need and then Frank would drop it in. This all went on for many years. Then Frank would do Betsy's food shopping for her on a Tuesday and a Friday. At one point, Betsy became particularly demanding, and Frank was nearly having a breakdown. I had to let her know that he was mentally unwell with stress. She backed off for a while, but it did not last long. Please do not feel too sorry for him, she was paying him very well for all these jobs.

Before we split up, I kept asking Frank when he was going to let Betsy know that we were splitting and he just could not seem to face it. By now, I was fond of her too, and I foolishly thought that I was important to her. Frank was also wearing his engagement and wedding ring all the time, which I found unsettling, but I do think it was so that people, like Betsy, would not ask him anything. By now, I had removed my wedding and engagement rings permanently. This was after I had thrown them at Frank a few times, telling him to give them to Melissa. I bought myself a ring for my wedding finger in the hope that all men would leave me alone forever and would think that I was married

So, when I moved out, I phoned Betsy and told her. I told her that Frank and I had split up and that we were getting divorced. I told her that Frank was having an affair with Melissa, to which she said, and I quote, "What, that ugly girl, who works with him in the taxi?" I agreed that would be her. I told her that we had sold our house and that Frank had moved and that I had moved. She sobbed like a baby! I sobbed. She said, "I am extremely disappointed in Frank, but you and I will still be friends." She said, "I will speak to him when he comes round." The next contact she and I had was hugely different. She was cold and heartless and did not want to know me, she said, "I need Frank to do my shopping!" So that was the end of that relationship too. How fickle.

Chapter 23

Back to when I saw Nick. Aside from my own pain and heartache, I was *so* angry! I was angry for what they had done to him. He was a good man who did not deserve this. I could recall Frank saying to me so many times, "Nick is my friend, and I would never hurt him." It was hard to reconcile that with what I now knew. Like I have said before, I had never seen another man look so lovingly at his wife as I had witnessed when Nick looked at Melissa. I was angry for what Frank had done to my children, what *they* had done to my children. My children had loved him so. I was angry that I had built relationships with his family, I loved them all, especially his children. I was angry that they broke up our happy family home. I was so angry that *she* had stolen my entire life.

From wanting to see Nick so desperately, I now saw him twice in a truly brief period. I was walking through the park one day, en route to my nail appointment, when I saw Nick walking toward me, taking their dogs for a walk. He confessed that he felt that Melissa and Frank's relationship had been going on longer than he first thought. I told him that I thought it had been going on for *much* longer than he thought! Unfortunately, I did not have the time to talk to him for long, but he did have time to tell me that they had been in my house when I was out. It was one body blow after another, the pain was relentless. What other revelations were there likely to be?

At night, I was tortured with images of Frank and Melissa having sex in my home while I was out. Not just having sex in my home, but anywhere. I would envisage them having sex all day and all night. It was driving me mental. As soon as I went to bed at night, I would see Frank's face and then would see them naked having sex. I had to try to shut my brain off, so that I could have some respite from the torment. I could see everything in my head in graphic detail.

One of the worst things throughout this whole experience had been the fact that Frank had 'gone off' me, sexually, because I had previously had breast cancer. But Melissa had suffered from it too, so I am assuming that she too had a wonky boob and a scar, the same as mine, but why did her surgery not affect him the same way that mine had? Was I so repulsive? I must have been a 'turn off' but she was obviously a 'turn on'. How did this work?

After I had found out about their shenanigans, of course, I phoned Frank, I am not made of wood with painted-on eyes. I told him exactly what I thought of him and, indeed, what I thought of them. All he could say repeatedly was, "I am sorry." I did ask how he was managing to 'get it up' and I did remind him that Melissa did not like sex. I told him that I thought they were a piece of low-life scum, which they were. He tried to tell me that he had 'only' been having sex with Melissa for seven weeks (oh great, that is okay then). Just hearing him say that sickened me to my soul. But Melissa had told Nick that she had 'only' been sleeping with Frank for five weeks. Like I said to him, neither of them could lie straight in bed.

When I was this angry, I felt like I could take on the world. I do not care how big you are, how many of you there are, or even if I fear you, I will still give it a go. My friend, Leigh, is always trying to calm me down, as he used to be the same, and he tells me to practice my 'inner zen'. Well, on this occasion, my 'inner zen' had well and truly packed its bags and left the building. Surely now you are beginning to understand why I killed her? I even found it offensive that she and I were breathing the same oxygen.

Rosie and I are remarkably similar, in every way. When Rosie was younger, a photographer stopped me in the street and said that he could tell that we were mother and daughter as we looked so alike, which we do. He asked if I would be interested in us doing some 'mother and daughter' photography work. I thought it would have been on the rough end of 'sleazy' so I declined. The only reason that I am telling you this is so that you know that, A) a man did find me attractive once, and, B) so you know that Rosie and I do look alike.

Not only do we look alike, but we also think alike, and we have both have ADHD. So, one Sunday afternoon, we were discussing what Frank and Melissa had done and we got ourselves so worked up that we decided to drive to Frank's new flat. We thought about buying a dozen eggs on the way and 'egging' his flat. We are nothing if not childish. Rosie had even discussed sending him some pig shit by post (this is a real thing if you too ever feel the need to let off some steam).

When we arrived at his flat, Melissa and Frank's matching red Lexuses were parked nose to tail under his window. Seeing this with my own eyes really brought home to me the fact that this was real and that they were spending their Sunday afternoon in flagrante delicto, and the blinds were shut. I nearly vomited into my own hands. We did not egg his flat, but Rosie and

I decided that this would be a suitable time to speak to Nick, as we knew for sure where Melissa was.

I knocked on the door and Nick answered. He did not seem overly shocked to see us. I asked if it would be all right to come in and talk to him. Obviously, my reputation of being a tad crazy had preceded me. I was snotty and crying and incredibly angry. Nick was cool, calm and collected. We could not be more different. He told Rosie and I that he loved Melissa and that he always had since school. Even when he said this, I could see him imagining her in his mind's eye and his eyes glazed over. I asked him if he was angry. He simply said that he did not want to be with someone that did not want to be with him. He said, "Well you did *know* Frank and Melissa were close." Yes, I did, but I was not happy with them playing tonsil tennis, never mind playing 'mummies and daddies', in my house!

Because Nick is such a gentle soul, he refused to get worked up. I really wanted him to get as angry as I felt, but it just was not happening. Most men would surely have wanted to kick Frank's head in? I mean, I would have held him down, if he had asked. Nick had even let Frank and Melissa 'play pool together' on their own, while Nick was in a different room watching TV. I will never understand why he thought that this was acceptable. How was he now surprised about what had happened? I know that Frank and Melissa would have told him that I was paranoid. Oh, Nick, why were you not a little more paranoid? I looked at Nick and wondered if I would be able to fancy him enough to have sex with him in a kind of 'revenge sex' way, but decided that I could not fancy a man who was this 'nice' and therein lies most of my problems...

I asked him if he had any idea what their long-term plans were. He said that he did not know, but that he would not divorce her and that he would also be refusing to move out of the house. He is a much better person than I am, as he was also not going to tell her dad, even though he lived with them, because he did not want to upset him, or tell his own dad, who used to come around for Sunday dinner every week. He said his dad 'adored Melissa'. I often wonder what these multitudes of men saw in this woman who was this worst kind of human.

Rosie told Nick that Frank was a womaniser and not to worry, as their relationship would not last. Nick said that Melissa had already told him that she had noticed a couple of 'red flags' about Frank anyway. I would simply love to know what they were, and so wish that I had remembered to ask her before I killed her. But, oh well. I told Nick about the eternity ring and the fact that Frank and I got back together in March, and he did look suitably triumphant! He said that Melissa did not know that, and I imagined, and was pleased, that Nick would be getting some joy out of telling her. It still does beg the question, though, why did Frank get back with me in March? Had he and Melissa fallen out? Was one of them getting cold feet?

He said that Frank had told Melissa that he had not told me that he loved me for 12 months. I was livid, as this was a blatant lie. When I got home, I went back over mine and Frank's WhatsApp messages, and he was so cunning that he had deleted every one of his messages saying that he loved me, so our 'chats' looked one-sided, with me being the only one to say 'I love you'. I offered to go out for a drink with Nick sometime and I gave him my phone number in case he ever needed somebody to talk to, but he never took me up on my offer. There was no need for you to fear me, Nick, you had not done anything wrong.

Unbelievably, because of them not wanting either father to know what was going on, Nick had agreed that, during the working day, Melissa would be able to come and go from the marital home and at night she could go and sleep with my husband. Nick allowed this! I envisaged her saying to him, "Bye, then, I am off out to have sex with my lover, see you in the morning." (I would have knee-capped her there and then). Also, during the weekend, she would be there on a Saturday to see her daughter and on a Sunday to cook the Sunday roast 'as usual'. *Please wake up, Nick!* And I have always wondered how Frank coped with her doing this. What if she was feeling bored with Frank and made overtures to Nick? The whole situation was mind-blowing.

I did not get the reaction that I wanted from Nick and never would. I forgot to add that whilst Rosie and I were on our rampage' we had James on the phone urging us to calm down, to 'please not do anything violent', and could we 'please stop acting like a pair of witches', as we were freaking him out. If you need someone to calm you down in a storm, please speak to my son, and if that fails, go to my friend, Leigh. Before you know it, you will be so zen, you will be horizontal. It does not actually work on me, but it is worth a try.

After we left Nick's, I immediately phoned Frank. I have never been so angry in my life, apart from at the climax of this story, and you know how that is going to end. I was apoplectic with rage. I told him that he and Melissa were the most disgusting and evil people I had ever come across, and various variations on that theme, with plenty of revolting swear words that are too much for me to even write down. Poor Rosie, she looked absolutely traumatised. I have never seen her look at me like that before, and I hope that she never does again. Astonishingly, Melissa had the brass neck afterwards to text me, 'How dare you come into my house'. Even recalling this is making my blood pressure rise! She had been in my house and was having sex with my husband. There really is nowt as strange as folk.

Chapter 24

I do not know what I ever did to upset Tilly. Or, indeed, what my children did. I know that Tilly was jealous of my relationship with her dad and then was jealous that Frank was living with two other children, which were not her or Bradley, and I do understand it. What I do not understand is the level of heartlessness that she was able to display, regarding some of her behaviour once Frank and I were no longer together. I guess the apple does not fall far from the tree. Firstly, there was the nasty email that she sent me before Christmas…

Then, just before I murdered Melissa, she put a photograph of her and Bradley with Frank and Melissa on social media of them all enjoying a meal together, knowing full well that poor James and Rosie would see it on Instagram. Dear of them, they were not going to tell me, but James and Rosie had both been really upset about it all weekend, and could not hold the pain in any longer. It was a very traumatic day indeed. I was *so* angry that my poor children were hurting again. This was *our* family once, and now we had to visibly see Melissa replacing us all. Not for the first time, I imagined killing her.

The photograph itself sickened me to my core. There was Melissa, with her blonde hair (the same colour as mine!), looking smug, like the cat that got the cream. At least Bradley had the decency not to look too impressed. I must say that Frank looked dreadful in the photo (I would like to think that is because he does have a conscience somewhere deep inside), but Tilly had a smile as wide as the Cheshire Cat's. I am guessing that she was happy to have her daddy back, but Melissa did not have a maternal bone in her body, so, I doubt Melissa would have actively encouraged him to make phone calls to them or arrange much contact.

On Frank's birthday, Rosie uploaded that photo just with Frank and Melissa enlarged, had a very jaunty rendition of 'Happy Birthday' sung over the top of it and on Frank's photograph, she had written, 'Dear Stepdad, I hope your birthday is as decent as you are as a stepdad, a parent, and a husband'. On Melissa she had written something along the lines of, 'And this inspirational woman, who has broken up even more marriages than even you have' (again, the apple does not fall far from the tree...). But it was all true, of course. I hope people will realise that this came from a place of deep emotional hurt. Frank has hurt my children more than he could ever know or be capable of understanding.

Tilly then sent Rosie a message saying that what Rosie had done had hurt her feelings, not acknowledging that putting up a photo of her dad with his new fancy woman might cause harm to James, Rosie, and myself. I cannot help but think that it was done with malice. Again, I will never understand what I ever did to Tilly to deserve this, and James and Rosie genuinely thought of Tilly as their sister. Just as I started to get over a very hurtful incident and start coming to terms with my situation, another painful incident or reminder would come along and bite me on the arse.

***

Just before Christmas, Dave H told me that his wife, Lesley, was dying. It was a really awful and tough time for him. I hope he won't mind me telling you that he was 'broken.' They had been together for over fifty years. Dave H and I spent a lot of time together then. He was suffering and I was suffering, and without each other, I am not sure that we would have even got through it. Sometimes, it takes tragedy to bring people together. Not in a romantic way necessarily, but in a way, that a true and lasting life-time friendship is born. Although Frank had not died and I cannot even begin to compare my situation with Dave's, I was still grieving for what to me, was a huge and irreplaceable loss.

Without Dave's support, I would not be where I am today. We have formed a friendship that is unique and one that I would never want to lose. Our friendship is not just based on our losses now, but also on a shared sense of humour, that I can only describe as outrageous! He is one of the funniest people that I have ever met and although we have had sad moments, I have also had some tremendous belly laughs with him. I am fully expecting him to visit me in here, and doubtless he will get thrown out, because our laughter won't go down very well with the screws.

**

It was so nice to have somebody on their own, like I was. Although I have a great deal of other friends, I am aware that they have their own lives and families. They are not just going to randomly phone me in the evening and say, "I am coming round for a coffee". Or, "Do you want to come to mine for a coffee tonight?" There are not enough adjectives to express the gratitude that I feel toward him. When he reads this, he will laugh out loud at my soppiness. Even imagining that is making me chuckle.

You must be wondering what my life looked like post-Frank and pre-me-killing-Melissa. Well, it was very, very different. For a start, living on your own can be a lonely business. However, it is not nearly as bad as I imagined it to be. I had an endless supply of visitors, so did not have to be on my own very much, but there was the odd day when, at the end of the day, I realised that I had not seen or spoken to a living soul. One thing that I did find strange was that all the males I knew were now expressing how much they thought of me, and how mad they thought Frank must have been for giving me up.

As nice and as flattering as that could sometimes be, at the beginning all I wanted was for Frank to realise that he had made a mistake and come back to me. It simply reinforced the fact that I had not been good enough for Frank's exacting standards and it was extremely detrimental to my own self-esteem. Men are still a bit stuck in the dark ages and in my experience still think that women are incapable of managing by themselves.

This means that every man you know will keep offering to help you, not realising that a woman can do all things that a man can do, like decorate, or hold a drill. Admittedly, we do not have the same physical strength, but being independent seems to make men feel emasculated and they offer to do it for you, not for one minute thinking that you are perfectly able. I could paint a ceiling or walls as good as any man, after all, I decorated my last home whilst Frank was entertaining his Lolita.

I no longer had a man expecting me to cook. I would ask myself, *what's for dinner?* and respond by opening a packet of Kettle crisps (usually mature cheddar and red onion flavour), pouring myself a large glass of Malbec and dessert would usually be a bowl of sweet and salty popcorn. Mmm, don't mind if I do. This was such a wonderful relief of duty and of obligation that I cannot recommend it highly enough. I genuinely think that it is good for your soul, if not for your waistline.

I have spent two thirds of my life being married and, as any woman will tell you, the worst part of marriage is thinking about, and then cooking, dinner. It feels like an eternity of thought, followed by action, and it is nothing short of mind-numbingly boring. You will be punished, though, by your friends and family nagging you that 'you are not eating properly', or saying, "You should look after yourself." But the trade-off is worth it. I highly recommend a Tesco 'meal deal', pasta or a sandwich with crisps and a drink. What's not to like? And no dishes!

There was only me now. Only my dirt. Only my washing and ironing. There used to be a pile of laundry that looked like a mountain, teetering over the edge of a precipice. But then, if I needed something ironing, well, I could iron as I went. I could sleep totally naked, and if it was hot I could lie spread-eagled on the bed, without anybody expecting me to have sex with them, or without anybody feeling violently sick. I could 'starfish' without punching my partner in the head and I could roll around with gay abandon.

There was no listening to snoring, or sleep apnoea, where your husband might stop breathing for several seconds and then you must lie there waiting for them to take a sudden and loud intake of breath, with you thinking that they were about to expire. I started to save money on not having to buy earplugs.

There was no farting, except my own (and I wondered why I could not get a boyfriend). There was no tussling over the bed sheets, they were all *mine*. I could do whatever I liked, whenever I liked. There was no arguing, only with myself. There was *peace*.

It is better to be miserable on your own, than to be miserable in a marriage. I would watch couples having a row, or doing that bickering thing that couples do, and simply think to myself, *thank God*. There is a lot of freedom in learning that you do not need another person to validate your existence. I also always tended to put my men on a pedestal, which is a mistake I will never make again. If I were to ever to be released, I would like the opportunity to do things differently, whether that was with, or without, a man.

***

When I first started living alone, Frank was incredibly good regarding the cats, and he was behaving honourably, regarding their welfare. Before I had moved out, I suggested that he just set up a direct debit of an agreed amount towards their keep, but he was not keen on doing that as he wanted some element of 'control' so instead suggested that anything I paid for the cats, I could just let him know and that he would pay half. He did not even ask to see receipts, though I offered. This was going very well for several months, and it was nice that it could be done amicably without any stress.

At some point (and I honestly cannot remember how I found this out), Tilly had given Frank one of her cats because I had 'taken' all our cats from him! He seemed happy for me to take our cats, so this, like a lot of things, doesn't make sense. It was not long before 'somebody' objected to him giving me money. Of course, this may have been Melissa, it may have been Tilly, or it may have been Frank's parents, but I guess I will never know. What I do know is that 'somebody' had told him that they did not feel that he should have to pay for cats that were no longer his. I used to send him photos and said that he could come and see them if he wanted to.

And so, what proceeded, I will now call 'cat-gate'. Unexpectedly, one day, Frank sent me a message saying, 'I am going to set up a standing order every month for the cats and then you won't have to send me itemised bills anymore'. We could not agree on an amount, and so proceeded a lot of toing and froing with questions as to what cat food I was feeding them, how much was I feeding them, could I buy food cheaper somewhere else, etc., etc. Well, I had known Frank for 18 years and I *knew* that 'somebody' was instructing him with what to write. His text messages were not even in his style of 'talking'.

He started to say how much money he had given me over a set period, along with sums he, or 'someone' had taken the time to work out. He then said, 'We are divorced. You kept all the cats and took 55 per cent of the house', and then I knew for sure that this was not Frank talking. He agreed that I would take the cats and he agreed that I could have 55 per cent of the house; this was 'someone' else objecting to me having money that *they* wanted. Fill in your own gaps here. I tried to phone Frank, but he would not answer. Whoever he was with had told him not to answer. Not for the first time, I wanted Frank to grow a pair. I mean, I know I'm scary, but please man up. He also had the nerve (or whoever was getting him to write it had), to say, 'A lot of people would not pay anything; they are your cats now'.

He told me that he had his own cat. Why would you take on another cat when you are already responsible for three others? He also told me that he had a rent increase. Even writing that has made my blood boil! Another lie is pending… But more later about that later. More Post-it notes! I was so incensed that I threatened to get some cat baskets and to drop them all at his flat. And when he said that he could not have four cats at his, I offered to drop them at Melissa's. As usual, he defended her, saying, 'This has nothing to do with her'. How could he think that? We would not even be having these 'cat wars' if it weren't for her! I must admit, I roared with laughter.

Chapter 25

My children started to come to terms with everything. My son, James, and daughter-in-law, Sofia, gave birth to a beautiful and amazing daughter, so I became a grandma, which is something that I had always wanted. It is an honour and a privilege to be a grandparent and a blessing that is far more precious than any man could ever have brought to my life. My daughter, Rosie, married Sammy and at my time of writing is about to bless me with the gift of yet another grandchild; this time, a grandson. These grandchildren of mine will be loved more than they will ever know. And even if they do not get to see me, I know that my love is strong enough to penetrate these walls.

Stefan stopped driving my taxi. I was sad to see him go. We had built up a great friendship and I nearly cried on our last journey. Alex replaced Stefan, another beautiful Romanian soul, who provided me with so much laughter that it was sheer joy to go to work every day. I continued to work with children with special needs and I loved them all dearly. I took on two other jobs, one cleaning and another being a personal assistant for McKenzie, who I used to take to school. He is a delight and his mum, Di, became a good friend. It was also freeing not to be dependant financially on a man. I would never put myself in that situation again either. If I ever get that chance.

Alex took over from Stefan in many ways, by also referring to Melissa as 'the gorilla' should we have seen her out driving her taxi. He referred to Frank, rather affectionately, as 'the monkey'. I never ever was able to control my anxiety or supress that feeling of bile rising whenever I saw either of their red Lexuses; but Alex did try to take the edge off by making me laugh. Bless him.

I often saw Daisy's father, who was also the operator for Frank's school run, parked up in his taxi by the local shopping centre. I decided one day to speak to him. He was also friends with Nick. I asked him if he knew that Frank and I had split up, and that Frank was now with Nick's wife. Much to my surprise, he did not know anything at all about it! But he did tell me that he had heard that Frank was moving back to the area. Again, just when I started to recover from the last devastating news, yet another set of circumstances would occur that would send me reeling.

My intuition kicked in and I *knew* exactly where Frank's new house was going to be. It was less than a ten-minute walk from where I was living. I found it hard to come to terms with the lack of his thought for me on this. By now, you would have thought that I would have become used to Frank's lack of thought for me! I found out for sure where he had moved to when my friend Donna's son, Daniel, moved a few hundred yards away. I went to have a look at Dan's new house and, sure enough, Frank's red Lexus was parked just around the corner.

I walked up to have a look at where he was now living several times. I was feeling a bit deranged again. I did not know if Melissa was also living there, until Dan told me that he had seen her coming out of the back gate. I made the huge mistake of walking around to see the front of the house (it was not visible from the road) and had the breath knocked out of me when I saw a huge 'Sold' sign outside. I could not believe my eyes! Yet another lie: "I will never buy another house."

This begged the question, how could he afford it? How did he get a mortgage at his age? And why lie? I then quickly realised that when we were arguing about cat-gate, he told me that his rent had gone up. The lying bastard was trying to cut down on his outgoings because he had a mortgage! The only thing that I could think of was that Tilly had sorted out his mortgage. Was she on the mortgage? Did she own some of the house? Were Nick and Melissa selling their house? Had Melissa gone on the mortgage? Well, there was only going to be one way to find out. I waited a few weeks and then ordered a copy of the deeds from the Land Registry… I know you are thinking: *Why bother? Does it matter now?* Well yes, it did to me. I am nothing if not nosey.

The next time that I saw Keith, I told him where Frank had moved to. I was so tempted to tell him about Frank's weird relationship with Daisy. Rosie could not believe that I didn't. As I saw Keith more frequently, I really struggled not to tell him. I think that all that prevented me was the fact that it would have really hurt him. I mean, he thinks that Frank is a nice guy. And Daisy does not deserve any grief or questioning as I do think that she was innocent. Also, it would mean telling him that his daughter was on some serious drugs. So, you see? I am a nice person.

Although it looked to all intents and purposes that Melissa and Frank were now living together full-time, there were still some very strange goings-on. For example, I would often walk past Nick and Melissa's house and her car would sometimes be outside. This might be during the day, or even late at night. I went round to see Diana and Patrick and she asked if there was any news because she thought Nick and Melissa were back together, as she had seen them out walking their dogs together. It was very puzzling.

Not long after I discovered that Frank had moved nearby, I did bump into him. He was dropping off some clients in the carpark of the shop I was going in. We were both in shock I think, though I had a sixth sense that I would see him soon. I said, "Hello." How limp? Is that how you greet someone that has destroyed your life? Well, it must be!

He said, "Hello." It was very awkward. How can it be awkward after you've seen each other naked? Anyway, I asked him if he was happy now (he looked dreadful and sad). He said, "There you go again, with your sarcasm," and rolled his eyes. He is the world's best eye-roller. On this occasion, I was being genuine. Because if that is how you look after you have run off with your fancy woman, then I wouldn't recommend it.

I said, "I am sorry I did not make you happy."

He said, "You did!"

WHAAATTT! I am obviously not cut out to understand men. I said, "I cannot believe that you have moved so close to me."

He said, "What difference does it make now?"

I said, "Well some people might think that it is rather cruel." (More eye-rolling). I said, "Do you want to talk?"

He said, "What about?" I mean, that is so outrageous, that it is quite funny.

What I really wanted towards the end was a proper decent conversation with my ex-husband. I did not feel that it was much to ask after 18 years. Obviously, I had to come to terms with the fact that this was never going to happen, and I would, indeed, never get any answers or closure. This was a bitter pill to swallow, as I am the type of person who needs clarity, otherwise my head is 'mashed'. I had hoped that we would have been able to talk amicably and to arrive at a mutual conclusion as to why our marriage had ended. I wanted us to both understand and to reach a peaceful conclusion as to what had happened.

As time went on, our current positions were more separate than they had ever been. Frank wanted to forget and move on, I wanted to talk it out, dissect it, and then move on. We were polar opposites in that regard. I felt we might both feel better if we at least met each other halfway. I knew that I had to forgive Frank for what he had done to me. I knew that it was not healthy to carry a grudge, they are a heavy burden that cannot be good for your soul. I felt that there was unfinished business, but that at some point, I would have to let it, and him, go if I were to ever recover. I still have many thoughts of Frank and those memories can still make me feel deeply sad, but I know that he has moved on with his life, and if I am ever to learn to love myself at all, then I had to give myself permission to be free and, in the future, maybe I could be happy with someone again.

I have been back to our old home, purely to visit our old neighbours, though, in general, it sickens me to have to walk past it, but I must make myself. Some of the neighbours told me that Melissa was there on the day that Frank moved out and that she was helping him. I won't lie, that really hurts. How could she be so brazen? Even the thought that she had walked where I had walked or touched anything that I had touched makes me feel violated. The neighbours could not believe it either and were also sad that, because we had lived there for so many years, thought Frank was their friend, and yet he did not say goodbye to one single one of them. I found myself apologising to them on his behalf.

Prior to this, I did speak to Frank a few times on the phone, but each time it felt like a mini-death. He also told me that my behaviour had forced him into Melissa's arms, so it was, and would always be, my fault, in Frank's opinion. He forgot to add that I also put a banana skin in front of him whilst he was out walking, and he slipped on it and fell right into Melissa's vagina. To conclude, I do not think that I will ever understand the man, so I decided to let him have his relationship with crusty knickers, without any more contact with me. At least that was until I ended her life.

Finale

Hopefully, by now, you will be able to fully appreciate the circumstances that have brought us to the conclusion of my story. I hope that from reading my account thus far you will accept with a clearer understanding that everything that has happened in my life reached a dramatic climax with what was to follow. In my eyes, at least, there was to be no other appropriate ending. There were times when I genuinely wanted to forgive Melissa. I wanted to forgive all those who had betrayed my trust and ultimately turned away from my love, as though it, and I, were worthless. Clearly, I did not have it in me.

Early one chilly morning, I decided to go for a walk. These times were where I did most of my thinking and praying. I was contemplating everything that had happened to me. It was the start of a bright autumnal day, with a hint of light showing through the trees. I like the autumn, particularly when the ground is covered in leaves of multicoloured shades of red and brown, which make a small crunchy sound as you walk over them. The path in front of me was scattered with them, along where I was walking.

I was feeling quite relaxed and at peace with myself. It had taken a long time to get to this point. I could remember the 'crying-walking' that I used to do, and was grateful that I had made it through that difficult time. I heard the train go by and recalled the many times where I felt like taking my own life. I even felt cheerful on that morning. My mind did not remain on my negative thoughts as I gradually became more aware of myself and my surroundings. I guess, in modern terms, I was 'mindful' and just 'living in the moment'. I imagined how pleased Rebecca would be if she could see how far I had come.

It was an unfortunate turn of events when just up ahead I spotted Melissa. I *knew* that it was her walking toward me, even though I had now not seen her for several months. She was, true to form, strutting along like a giant peacock. Her bleached hair (an attempt to even take my hair colour from me) was the only thing that looked different from how I had seen her at the start of this, when she wanted to see if she could successfully steal my husband, and she had. I could also see that she, too, had noticed me now. That familiar feeling of bile rising from my abdomen right up into my throat started to do its thing, but I managed to swallow and supress it.

My first instinct was to run from her, but I was determined not to show any fear so I proceeded to walk with purpose. She turned off the path just in front of me, which lead in the direction of the park, but not before she glared at me with the hatred that I had seen so many times before. She had won, so I still do not know why she had to glare. She should not have glared... My fear of her now had turned to anger – not just ordinary anger, I was so enraged that I could feel my blood pumping through my veins. There was a sensation of complete and utter abandonment of any self-restraint, the like of which I had never before encountered.

I picked up my speed and that was when I spotted a piece of wood in the undergrowth that looked like a piece of broken fence post. At that moment – and you may not believe me – I picked it up and had not planned or even thought about what

I was going to do with it. It was like somebody or something had taken over my body and mind and I was no longer in control of my faculties. I know that I did enjoy the feel and the weight of that piece of wood in my hand. It was in good condition; it just felt a bit damp from where it had been lying in the soil and the wet leaves.

There was nobody in the park that day, not one solitary person. It was still early and the atmosphere was eerily quiet. The dew on the grass was starting to evaporate in the sunlight, creating a fine mist. I really felt quite serene. I continued to walk at speed now, but as stealthily as I could. It was lucky that I was wearing trainers. I then decided to run and as I did so, I raised that piece of wood as high up as I could, holding it with both hands, and then I smashed it onto the top of Melissa's head, as hard and as fast as I possibly could. In that quiet park it made such a loud thud as the wood and her skull made contact.

Melissa put her hands up to defend herself and she let out a blood-curdling scream, but she did not go down yet. She still looked cocky, and I swear she gave me a sly grin, so I swung that wood repeatedly: Thud! Thud! Thud! I didn't even focus on what I was hitting as the adrenalin soared through my veins, and then she dropped to her knees, cowering. It certainly, made a change, who was frightened of whom, now?

As I tried to focus, I could see that she had blood trickling slowly out of one of her ears. I was getting tired now, my adrenalin had reached its pinnacle and was starting to subside a little. My fingers hurt from gripping so hard, and my arms were aching. On my final strike with the wood, I gave everything that I had left, and I smashed it into her face.

What was left of her nose left blood cascading out of both nostrils. I could smell fresh metallic blood on the slight autumn breeze.

I pushed Melissa over; it only took a slight nudge of my foot, and she was flat on the ground. I was getting so cross now; what was it going to take to kill this bitch? I dropped the wood, and then I continued to punch her over and over with my fists. All the pain of my betrayals, all my rejection and all my suffering enabled me to pummel and pummel her face and body until all suddenly stilled. Then, for the first time, I surveyed the carnage in front of me. I had not realised that the wood must have had a nail poking out of the end of it; it had caused more damage than I had expected. Melissa's clothes were all ripped and bloodied, and the nail had made puncture wounds all over her body.

I knew that Melissa was already dead, but I continued to inflict further blows upon her body. Every body blow was for somebody she had hurt – for Nick, for James, for Rosie, for me, for the rest of my family. Melissa and Frank had hurt so many people, without a thought for anybody else, but just to satisfy their own selfish lust. My anger was not fully sated until I could see her innards laid bare and her entrails were lying like motionless snakes upon the grass.

Afterward, I was spent and exhausted. I felt like I just needed to sleep. But I also felt free, happy and elated! To say that my emotions were confused is an understatement. I did not care about the consequences of what had just occurred, not even for a second. This was not the sort of murder you could even try to get away with – I like to think that I had motive. I thought about handing myself in to the police station, but then remembered that our local police station was closed. This would mean a trip into town then, and I really could not be bothered. What could I do? Get on a bus covered in bits of Melissa? I did think the police might be glad of something juicy to get their teeth into, so in some respects surmised that I was doing them a bit of a favour. No, I decided, I would go home for a shower, so at least I would look a little smart when they came to arrest me.

I kicked the post back into the undergrowth. The irony was not lost on me that I had killed Melissa with the very thing that had been used for Frank's hobby, but which he had to get rid of once she turned our lives upside down. I did have a little chuckle. I wonder what Frank would do now, without his woodwork and without Melissa... I could see that the post was thick with blood, hair and fragments of bone. My own DNA would be all over everything. There was blood spatter galore for the entertainment of the forensic pathologists; all in all, it had turned out to be a good day for everyone.

Melissa lay in a crumpled and bloodied mess on the ground, and I was totally covered in her blood – it felt warm and sticky. I was surprised that her blood looked normal, as most of the time I did not even see her as a human being. I did not see one other person in the park that morning, but I figured somebody somewhere would have seen something, as there were houses overlooking the park. I wondered how long it would take me to get arrested. It is *so* tiring killing somebody that way. I would not recommend it. My whole body was burning and aching. I have suffered with osteoarthritis in my hands for some years, and could feel every bone and every joint in my fingers throbbing.

I walked home slowly, the full magnitude of my crime not fully registering. I did feel a bit like a child at Christmas; I had been given one of the best presents I would ever have and I had not even asked for it, nor had I been expecting it! I was feeling so joyous. I realise that you may think badly of me, but I hope, also, that you will find it in your hearts to be a little bit pleased for me. It is not very often in this life that you see injustice rectified in such a spectacular fashion.

I hope that you, the people, will realise that I did this not just for me, but for all those men, women and children who have been affected by somebody they love making them feel rejected, alone, betrayed or gaslighted, by the one person whom they thought loved them above all else. You may be thinking it unfair that Melissa has taken the brunt of all my anger. After all, it takes two to tango and nobody forced Frank to betray me – he could, and should, have resisted. I can, however, excuse his behaviour a little, as Melissa had been so good and talented in what she did.

Why do you think God used Eve to tempt Adam? Because even He knows how easily men can be manipulated by a woman's allure. Frank's punishment will be that he no longer has Melissa, and he had given up his whole life just to be with her. To think he wondered why I said she must be magnificent. So, going forward, he now has nothing.

Let's see how he likes it…

About the Author

Denise Shaw lives happily in Plympton, Devon. She is man-free, but that is how she likes it! She enjoys the company of her three cats. She has two children and two grandchildren whom she adores.

This is her second book.

9 781803 819129